NEW KIND OF GUNPLAY

Ruff Justice had looked into the wrong end of a gun before—but never like this.

The gun was a Winchester in the hands of a beautiful Indian girl who had stripped off her clothes to reveal one of the greatest bodies Ruff had ever seen.

Going to where Ruff's previous companion, Ada Sinclair, had left intimate things scattered when fleeing the room, she picked up a petticoat.

"Who would wear these things?" she asked, throwing it down. Then she turned to Ruff, who lay still naked on the bed. "Ready to prove yourself, man of legend?"

"With a gun on me?" Ruff said.

The woman shrugged. "A gun is worth much. It purchases many things."

"Better drop it," said Ruff. "For what I've got in mind, that damn thing will only be in the way. . . ."

RUFF JUSTICE #27

The Thunder Riders

by

Warren T. Longtree

A SIGNET BOOK

NEW AMERICAN LIBRARY

PUBLISHED BY
THE NEW AMERICAN LIBRARY
OF CANADA LIMITED

PUBLISHER'S NOTE

This novel is a work of fiction. Names, characters, places, and incidents either are the product of the author's imagination or are used fictitiously, and any resemblance to actual persons, living or dead, events, or locales is entirely coincidental.

The first chapter of this book appeared in *Twisted Arrow*, the twenty-sixth volume in this series.

First Printing, August, 1986

2 3 4 5 6 7 8 9

SIGNET TRADEMARK REG. U.S. PAT. OFF. AND FOREIGN COUNTRIES
REGISTERED TRADEMARK — MARCA REGISTRADA
HECHO EN WINNIPEG, CANADA

SIGNET, SIGNET CLASSIC, MENTOR, ONYX, PLUME, MERIDIAN AND NAL BOOKS are published in Canada by The New American Library of Canada, Limited, 81 Mack Avenue, Scarborough, Ontario, Canada M1L 1M8

PRINTED IN CANADA
COVER PRINTED IN U.S.A.

RUFF JUSTICE

He knew the West better than any man alive—a hostile, savage land rife with both violent outlaws and courageous adventurers. But Ruff Justice had a sixth sense that kept him breathing and saw his enemies dead. A scout for the U.S. Cavalry, he was paid to protect the public, and nobody was faster at sniffing out a killer, a crook, a con man—red or white, at close range or far. Anyone on the wrong side of the law would have to reckon with the menace of Ruff's murderously sharp stag-handled bowie knife, with his Colt pistol, and the Spencer rifle he cradled in his arms.

Ruff Justice, gentleman and frontier philosopher—good men respected him, bad men feared him, and women, good and bad, wanted him with all the wildness of the Old West.

1

She had a gun but she wasn't quite ready to use it. The tall man in buckskins was just stepping out of his trousers, crossing the room toward the bed, his silhouette lean and masculine in the light of the low-burning lantern on the hotel table.

Outside, Bismarck, Dakota Territory, continued its night of drinking and gambling, carousing and violence. Inside, the bed was soft and warm, the sheets forming themselves around the contours of the blond woman's lush body.

The senator's daughter looked up at the tall man who stood beside the bed, naked and hard. His hair was long and dark, brushed down across his scarred shoulders; his mouth curved wickedly beneath his drooping black mustache.

Ada Sinclair reached out and let her hand grope upward from the tall man's thigh to his erect manhood. "What are you waiting for?" she asked.

She scooted to the far side of the bed, feeling the hard bulge of the Colt revolver beneath her pillow. The revolver she would use to stop the tall man's heart.

Later.

Later, after he had finished climbing on her, kissing her throat and breasts and thighs, her soft, flat abdomen, her hungry full lips. It seemed a shame but they said it had to be done. What a waste of manhood.

Ruff Justice was his name, and he was built long and lean and angular with ropy muscles, a solid stomach, and hard-muscled thighs. He was a scout and a frontiersman, a hunter and a lover of women—he knew all of his crafts well.

The senator's daughter lifted the sheet and Ruff Justice crawled in beside her to place his naked, needful body next to hers, to let his callused hands run across her breasts, teasing the taut pink nipples, dropping to her slender, sleek thighs.

Ada's breath began to come rapidly. She lay dreamily against the pillow, arm thrown limply to one side, waves of long golden hair fanned out against the pillowcase. Her eyes half-closed, lips half-parted as the tall man methodically worked his way over her body with probing fingers and hungry mouth.

The senator had come west a few months back to look into the situation on the plains. Back East, some were still crying for the army to avenge Little Big Horn, others screaming that the plains tribes had had enough—that they ought to be offered an honorable peace and the United States ought to stick by it.

On the plains of Dakota, too, there were a lot of people who had been hurt by the Sioux and the Cheyenne and were now demanding that every last "wild" Indian be buried beneath the prairie; while others thought that the war would never end unless a just treaty was signed.

Rather than listen to speech makers and headline writers, and the often incoherent letters of his constituents, Senator Cotton Sinclair had done what few others were willing to do. He had gotten up from his desk, stepped on a train, and come out to see for himself what in hell was happening.

As a bonus he had brought his daughter west, and Ada

Sinclair was justification enough for the senator's existence. She was sleek, cultured, beautiful beyond the dreams of most plainsmen, full breasted and so slender at the waist that Justice could place his hands around her there. Blessed with firm, flaring hips that swayed hypnotically when she walked, she didn't draw the usual collection of jeers, whistles, remarks, and catcalls when she strolled through Bismarck twirling her parasol. The men just stood and stared in sheer disbelief.

If she was something dressed, on the street, she was much more in bed: hungry for love, sleek and compelling, her kisses practiced and eager, her body a dream meant to comfort a needful man.

She lifted her hands now and her fingers ran lightly over Justice's hard buttocks, drawing him nearer to her before she lifted and spread her knees with a sigh, offering him the sanctuary of her warm, tender body.

"I didn't thank you for showing me Bismarck," Ada Sinclair said. Her fingers had wrapped around Ruff's shaft and now she gently guided him in, teasing him.

"Orders," Justice said. "Your father has some pull with the colonel, you know."

"Is *this* orders?" she asked, arching her back, holding his hand to her full breast, smiling up out of the depths of her pleasure as Justice penetrated another fraction of an inch.

"Sure, that's the only time I'd ever do something like this," Ruff Justice said. He kissed her neck beneath her ear, smelling the faint, haunting scent of her perfume.

"Orders," she said from far away. Her hands wrapped around his neck and she clung to him, pressing her body against his, her pelvis striking out hungrily. "Here's an order—deeper, Ruff, give it to me. Fix it for me."

Breathed into his ear, the order was an easy one to follow. Justice fell into a tangle of love with the blonde, rolling from side to side, arms and legs clutching, mouths clinging to flesh. Justice's rhythm, deep and insistent, brought cries of joy from the lips of the senator's daughter until with a last, nearly anguished gasp she reached a solid, trembling climax.

"God, that's why I came west, that's why . . ."

Justice still swayed against her, tasting her breasts, her sweet full lips. She stroked his long dark hair, looking up at him with pleasure and a sort of feminine pride from the depths of her emerald-green eyes.

She felt him tense, sway against her, felt his body thrust against her one final time before he found his release, rolling her onto her back to hover over her and look down at her, arms braced, eyes searching.

"What would your commanding officer say?" Ada asked, her finger tracing a pattern across Justice's solid chest.

"What would your father say?" Justice asked, bending low to kiss those full, warm lips again.

"My father wouldn't say anything. He'd simply have you shot," Ada Sinclair answered.

"Would he, now? You come from a violent family."

"Yes, we . . ." But the smile faded from her lips and from her eyes.

Justice wondered what deep nerve he had touched with the remark. He lowered himself again to lie beside her, feeling her occasional tight embrace, the searching of her hands, the light kiss that came from time to time as he began to doze into a satisfied sleep.

Ada Sinclair sighed, let her finger run along the tall man's eyebrow toward his ear. Then she kissed her finger and touched it to that ear.

It was a shame, she thought, such a goddamn shame. She looked at the moon peering in through the window of their ground-floor hotel room, watching its dull sheen for a time. Then she removed her left hand from Ruff's shoulder, alert for any sign that the man was not asleep.

Her hand went under her pillow and her fingers touched

the smooth walnut grips of the big Colt revolver there, slowly wrapping around it.

Ada glanced again at the window and at the one opposite. Beside that window sat a chair with her clothes on it. It was there that Justice had seated her and had slowly begun undressing her: unbuttoning her shoes, removing her stockings, each step followed by a kiss—on her calf, her thigh as he worked his way upward, on her shoulders and breasts as he undid her dress and slid it from her.

There was a man who knew how to make love. He acted as if he had no place else to go, nothing else on his mind. That the world had begun and ended in this room with this act . . . It was truly a shame to have to kill Ruff Justice.

Ada lifted her thigh from Justice's carefully, watching his nose twitch once, his fingers clench. Then she was away from him, out of the bed, standing naked over the army scout, the huge Peacemaker in her hands, cocked and ready to fire.

"Good-bye, Ruff Justice," the senator's daughter said under her breath. "Sorry."

The glass in the window before her was smashed out by a rifle barrel and Ada Sinclair shifted her aim, jerking the gun upward as she yanked too hard on the trigger. The bullet flew into the wall, scattering plaster everywhere. From the window an answering bullet was fired, narrowly missing Ada's head.

Ruff Justice had rolled from the bed, reaching automatically for his holstered pistol, which he had hung on a bedside chair, but the pistol was gone.

He saw Ada Sinclair, naked, gun in hand, ducking low as she moved across the hotel room toward the opposite window.

"Ada," Justice called out, and as he did, the woman swung the muzzle of her pistol toward him. Justice ducked below the bed as the Colt revolver spat flame and a .44

slug ripped its way through mattress and bed frame, leaving the bedding smoldering.

Then Ada was at the window, stepping over the sill as she grabbed for the dress she had left behind, sending another wild shot toward the window opposite.

Plaster flew and the gun's report echoed through the room. A cloud of black powder smoke hung over the bed. Ada was gone. The window curtains moved lightly in the evening breeze and Justice heard several light footsteps as the senator's daughter made her escape up the alley.

Puzzled and angry, Justice rose and walked to the far window. The breeze was cool against his naked body. He found his empty holster under Ada Sinclair's petticoats, but his pistol was nowhere to be seen. Presumably it was his own gun that the woman had fired at him.

"Why?" Justice asked himself. It made no sense at all. Ada Sinclair had come to town, a visiting dignitary, allowed herself to be taken to Justice's bed, and had apparently enjoyed what had followed.

"Maybe you've lost your touch," Justice muttered. He slammed the window shut and turned. As he did, the woman with the dark hair and Indian eyes came in through the other window.

She had a Winchester repeater in her hands and wore her hair tied back with a piece of rawhide string. She had on a white blouse, leather vest, and leather divided skirt. A length of golden leg showed itself as she stepped over the sill.

Ada Sinclair had worn corset, petticoats, chemise, and pantaloons under her clothing. It had taken Justice a long while to get them all off.

This one wore nothing beneath her blouse. Dark nippled breasts jutted against the white fabric so clearly that she might as well have worn nothing. Her legs were long, her mouth sensual yet firm.

She carried the Winchester low, the muzzle pointed at Ruff's belly.

"You have the right room, lady?" Justice asked. He stood naked, one hand on the wall, eyeing her closely. She looked around the hotel room cautiously, coming forward another stride.

"You are Ruff Justice?" she asked. There was an accent to her voice and Justice knew then what she was. He had heard Cheyenne Indians speak before.

"That's right," he replied.

"Army scout. Man of legends."

Ruff smiled. "Army scout."

"Man of legends," the Indian woman insisted.

"Maybe. Have you come to kill me, Cheyenne woman?" he asked in her own tongue.

"Not you," she answered in English. "Not to kill you, but now that I am here, I want to know." Her eyes roamed over his body, pausing with interest at his crotch. "I want to see if you are the man the legends say."

Then she opened her blouse with one hand, nearly popping the buttons as her honey-colored breasts bobbed free of their thin covering.

"Show me now, man of legend, or I will have to shoot you."

2

Justice backed away a step, looking at the woman. She was serious, dead serious, and the Winchester in her hands didn't brook much argument.

"You don't care to tell me what all this is about, do you?" Justice asked.

"Man of legend knows well enough what it is about." The Cheyenne girl untied a rawhide band from her hair with one hand and shook her long blue-black hair free.

"I mean the shooting," Ruff Justice said. There was a faint smile on his lips, but his eyes were wary, looking for some indication on the woman's face as to what she wanted.

There seemed to be only one thing on her mind at the moment—but at gunpoint?

"None of that concerns you. The white woman is gone. Too bad she is not dead, but she is gone." The Cheyenne stepped from her skirt, circling the room, her legs long and sleek. She went to where Ada Sinclair had left her clothes, picked up a petticoat with one hand, and examined it, her lower lip thrust out.

"Who could wear these things?" she asked, throwing it down again. Then she demanded abruptly, "Are you ready?"

"With a gun on me?"

The woman shrugged. "A gun is worth much in this world. It purchases many things."

"What band are you?" Justice asked suddenly, and the woman's eyes lifted. "Who is your chief?"

"It doesn't matter. Lie down, man of legend, Ruff Justice. Lie down or I will shoot you. You are going to make love to me as you did to the white woman. Or I will shoot you."

There wasn't much of a choice. Besides, as she crossed the room, nude and agile, her breasts high and full, the dark triangle at the juncture of her thighs ripe and summoning, Justice wasn't all that sure the Cheyenne woman needed a gun at all. She was young and eager. The circumstances might have been bizarre, but Ruff felt his desire growing. What the hell, he decided, you can't fight it.

He stretched out a hand and the woman brought the muzzle of her Winchester up sharply. Justice took the barrel of it, locking eyes with the Cheyenne. Then he ripped it from her hands and tossed it aside, to clatter against the floor.

"For what I've got in mind that damn thing will definitely be in the way," Justice said.

She hesitated, then frowned. Finally, her eyes lighting, she slipped in beside him and Justice tugged her to him. He was right—that damned rifle would have been in the way.

He awoke with the sunlight streaming through the curtained, broken window of the hotel room, to find the Cheyenne girl and her rifle gone. A contingent of soldiers—three of them—were standing around his bed.

Corporal Bill Bell was there and a private Ruff didn't know, gripping his Springfield rifle tightly, his eyes alert and maybe a little scared. The man in charge was Sergeant Ray Hardistein, an old friend, but he didn't look real friendly just then. In Hardistein's hand was a petticoat.

"You want to get dressed, Mister Justice," Hardistein said.

"*Mister*? When'd you get so formal, Ray?"

"Please, Mister Justice," the soldier repeated.

Ruff shrugged and rolled out of bed, crossing naked to where his clothing lay. He noticed that his sheathed Spencer rifle had been moved nearer the door.

"What's the trouble, Ray?" Ruff asked, stepping into his buckskin trousers.

"I think you know. Just get dressed, all right?"

"The colonel send you?"

"Get dressed," Hardistein repeated.

It was only after Justice had pulled on his shirt and tugged his boots on that Hardistein produced the manacles.

"Forget it," Justice said.

"I'd put 'em on if I were you," Hardistein said.

"No." Justice's voice had lowered and become steely. "I'll go along with you wherever you like, Ray, but I won't go in manacles."

"Orders," the sergeant said.

"To hell with your orders. There's two ways you can have this Ray: we walk out together and I go along nicely to wherever you say, or you and these two try putting those things on me by main force."

"Don't think we can't do it, Mister Justice. I know you're a fighter, but we've done a little on our own."

"Ray," Ruff Justice advised the NCO, "you'll have to shoot me to get those things on me."

Hardistein locked eyes with Justice. The sergeant took a long time thinking it over, but finally he nodded, putting the manacles away on a belt ring. "All right," he said. "But I'll tell you this, Justice: if you try to run, by God, we *will* shoot you."

"Thanks, Ray," Justice said sourly.

"I'm sorry, Ruff . . . Dammit, it's orders."

"Sure." Justice picked up his gray stetson with the yellow scarf tied around it, wiped back his long dark hair, and planted his hat. "Let's go, then."

There were a lot of lookers-on in the hotel hallway, the manager of the place among them. The three soldiers formed themselves around Justice and they tramped down the hall. Hardistein still held the petticoat, which caused some muttering and not a little tittering.

Hardistein growled something; a man Ruff knew called out, "They finally caught you at it, Justice?" and laughed. Ruff didn't smile in return.

Outside, the day was cold and clear. There had been a frost overnight and the main street still held white ridges where the mud hadn't been churned up by early-morning traffic. The soldiers and their prisoner crossed the street, stepped up onto the opposite boardwalk, and continued on past gawkers and surprised matrons. Now and then someone jeered or called out to Justice.

"Here," Ray Hardistein said as they reached the Masonic lodge.

"Not the fort?" the scout asked.

"Here," Hardistein said again.

One of the soldiers opened the heavy varnished door to the lodge, and Justice strode up the stone steps and in. They crossed the polished wooden floor to a stairway and started up.

"What's going on, Ray?"

"I guess they'll tell you," the sergeant answered.

Ruff gave it up. Hardistein seemed to be performing, acting especially tough so that he couldn't be accused of letting friendship get in the way of duty.

Justice asked, "Want me to put those manacles on, Ray?"

Hardistein's mouth tightened. "Forget it, Ruffin. All they can do is take my stripes." Then his stiffness returned. His jaw clamped shut and he walked on, heavily, silently, clutching the petticoat that belonged to the senator's daughter.

They reached a doorway at the end of the hall and Hardistein halted his men, stepping forward to rap on the door. The voice from inside was that of Fort Lincoln's commanding officer, Colonel MacEnroe.

"Enter," he said, his voice as stern and inflexible as an accusing high priest's.

Ruff glanced at Hardistein, who nodded, and Justice opened the door, preceding his escort into the room.

There were two men in the room, which contained an unslept-in bed, a massive desk, and three high-backed mahogany chairs. Colonel MacEnroe sat rigidly in one of these chairs, his hat on his lap, his face gray with anger. His eyes flickered to Justice and then to Hardistein, focusing briefly on the manacles at the sergeant's waist. Hardistein stepped forward, saluted, and placed the petticoat on the huge desk where the second man sat.

"Prisoner Ruffin T. Justice, sir," Hardistein said.

"Take up your post in the hallway, Sergeant," MacEnroe said as if it were painful to move his lips.

Justice watched him, waiting for the colonel to explode, for his face to flush with color, but he simply sat there. Hardistein and his men retreated to the hallway. Justice removed his hat and waited as the second man, the man at the desk, fingered the petticoat and glared at Ruff with dark-brown, feral eyes.

Senator Cotton Sinclair had a massive head of curled white hair rising from a round skull. His nose was slightly bulbous, the result of an old injury. His hands were red and raw, the skin on his neck beginning to sag. As the door closed behind Justice, he continued to sit there, glaring. Finally in a voice like one from a crypt he asked, "Where is my daughter, Mister Justice?"

"I couldn't say," Ruff Justice answered, and the senator's grip tightened on the petticoat.

"You slept with her."

"Not much," Ruff answered dryly, and the senator sprang from his chair, fists clenched, face purple with rage. He rounded the desk, holding one fist high.

"I wouldn't do that, sir," Justice said.

"I'll beat you to pulp!"

"Not alone you won't," Justice promised him.

"Do you know who I am?"

"Sure, an old man who's lost his daughter. Let's talk about it. I damn sure won't let you hit me, Senator, and you won't like the results if you try."

"Justice!" This was Colonel MacEnroe, an army officer who wouldn't dream of striking at a United States senator, or of talking back to one.

"MacEnroe!" Sinclair turned on the army colonel. "Order this civilian scout to tell me what he knows about my daughter's disappearance."

"Nobody has to order me to do that, Senator," Justice said mildly. "But threats aren't going to do any good. I didn't even know Ada *was* missing. I'll tell you anything I can about it."

"You slept with her," the senator said as if Ruff had cut his daughter's fine white throat.

"I told you that. Remember, she slept with me too."

"Justice," the colonel said, looking pained. "Discretion—couldn't you have used some discretion? For once?"

"It seemed to be between the two of us," Justice said.

No one responded to that. The senator ran a hand across his woolly head of white hair, returned to his desk, and sagged into the chair. Sorrowfully he said to MacEnroe, "This is the man you chose to guide my daughter around Bismarck."

MacEnroe didn't respond. The senator had begun fingering the petticoat again. His eyes had softened, reddened.

"Where is she?" he asked Justice.

"I told you I don't know."

"You . . . slept with her, and when you awoke, she was gone?" the senator asked.

"Not exactly," Justice replied, and he told them how it had been. "Sometime in the middle of the night your daughter lifted my revolver and tried to kill me with it."

"Why?"

"I couldn't say."

"That's preposterous," the senator said coldly. "Ada tried to shoot you? What had you done to her?"

"Nothing new or unusual," Justice said in a way that infuriated the senator still more.

"She shot at you?" MacEnroe asked numbly. He had always trusted his civilian scout, although he had long known of Ruff Justice's ways with women. Justice had enraged him in the past, but this was something different: a senator had come to look into the Indian situation, bringing his lovely young daughter, and Justice had seduced her. Now he was accusing the woman of trying to murder him—without knowing why.

"She shot at me. And missed." Justice rubbed his jaw. "Someone in the window took a shot at her and she fled."

"Someone in the window?"

"A woman. Indian woman," Justice said.

"Come now, Justice," Senator Sinclair exploded. "Your tale is not only ludicrous but insulting."

"Can't help that." Ruff shrugged. "That's what happened."

"And this Indian girl, what became of her? You slept with her as well, I suppose," the senator said with deep sarcasm.

"At gunpoint," Ruff answered.

The two older men just stared at him.

"Ruffin," the colonel said, rising, "why didn't you follow the senator's daughter and try to find her?"

"I told you someone had a gun on me. Besides, just

because Ada was crazy enough to run through the streets of Bismarck naked didn't mean I was."

"Damn you!" The senator's fist rose and fell, crashing against the solid desk. "Damn you for a liar and a scoundrel! I can't accept a word of this fabrication. You want me to believe my daughter made love with a man she barely knew, tried to kill him for no reason whatever, and then was chased away by an Indian girl who somehow appeared to protect you from her murderous intent? The tale, Justice, is not only fatuous but incredible."

"Sure," was all Ruff Justice said in response.

"What really happened?"

"I told you."

"Where is Ada Sinclair? Did you try to rape her?" the colonel asked.

"Sure," Ruff Justice replied. His eyes showed disappointment in Colonel MacEnroe, a man he had guided, fought beside, and slept beside on many occasions—a man whose life he had saved.

"Where is the body, Justice?" the senator asked, and Justice just shook his head, not knowing which of them was mad. The events of the night before had had a dreamlike unreality about them, but he was sure what had happened—he had been there.

"Still running loose, still naked, for all I know," he muttered after a minute.

The senator rose again, but abruptly turned away as if worried about what he might do to this tall, mustached army scout.

Colonel MacEnroe strode purposefully to the door, opened it, and said, "Sergeant Hardistein, escort Mister Justice to the stockade."

"The stockade, sir?"

"That's what I said, Sergeant, and by God, I want those manacles on him." He turned to Ruff. "Unless Justice wants to abandon this ridiculous canard and tell us where Ada Sinclair is and what happened to her."

Justice had too much of his own fury in him just then to answer. He only shook his head, thrust out his hands toward Hardistein, and waited while the sergeant locked the manacles on.

"Let's go," Hardistein said, and Justice turned toward the door, walked into the corridor and down the stairs. Outside, a small knot of curiosity-seekers watched as Justice was led to where three army bays stood beside Ruff's little zebra dun horse.

"Ruff," Ray said with something like apology in his voice, "can't you tell them what happened?"

"I told them, Ray. They don't like the story."

"If that girl shows up dead . . ."

"I know," Justice answered. "I know."

"I'd hate like hell to see you in front of a firing squad."

"Don't worry, Ray," Justice said with a quick grin, "they hang civilians, you know."

"Yeah." Hardistein wasn't in the mood for dark humor. They watched as Justice swung aboard his dun, manacled hands on the pommel. Then the soldiers mounted and led Ruff Justice up Bismarck's muddy main street toward Fort Lincoln and the stockade.

The warder was a dour man named Albertson who seemed never to have seen sunshine. He searched Justice again, filled out a few papers, which Hardistein signed as well, and led Justice to a small, dark cell. The iron door clanged shut, echoing through the cell block. Then Albertson asked for Justice's hands and unlocked the manacles.

Slowly, heavily, Albertson walked away, leaving Ruff Justice to examine his cramped quarters.

An iron bed frame with a flimsy ticking mattress hung from chains on one wall. Blue light streamed through the tiny high window of the cell, forming a bent wedge where it met the opposite wall and the stone floor. The sounds of the fort echoed distantly: sharp commands, horses walking in broken rhythm.

Ruff jumped up, gripped the bars of the window, and peered out, seeing the stockade wall beyond. On the ground below it an armed trooper was dutifully pacing off his shift. The bars were tight, very tight.

Justice dropped to the ground again and turned toward the iron door. Down the hall a trooper with the d.t.s cried out something unintelligible to a betraying Bacchus.

Slowly Sergeant Albertson stumped down the corridor toward him, glancing at Ruff as he passed. Justice went to the bunk and sat on it, his eyes fixed on the window above him. No one had ever broken out of the Lincoln stockade, and Justice had no hope of being the first.

And once outside, where could he go? Ruff didn't bother thinking about it just then. He lay back, hands clasped behind his head. Sooner or later Ada Sinclair would show up half-dressed, and if she told the truth about things, the colonel would spring Justice.

The senator would cool down after he had time to reflect on things and realize his baby daughter was a grown woman. He might not like what had happened, but he would get used to it. Besides fornicating, what did they have on Justice? And, he considered, if a man could be held in the stockade for that, there wouldn't be enough soldiers left outside to guard the ones inside. He yawned and stretched out, waiting.

It was dusk when they came: a grim-faced Colonel MacEnroe, Sergeant Hardistein with a rifle in hand, and Albertson with his plodding step and heavy iron ring of keys.

Ruff sat up, glanced at the window, where purple light colored the evening sky, and waited while Albertson unlocked the cell door.

MacEnroe entered; Hardistein stayed outside with his

rifle raised just enough to let Justice know he was watching. Albertson stood by like a man lost between life and death.

"Found her?" Ruff asked, fighting back another yawn.

"That's right," the colonel said slowly.

"Well? The senator still want me locked up?"

"Yes, Justice, he does."

"What's the charge, then, Colonel?" Ruff asked with a slight smile, a smile that faded with Colonel MacEnroe's studied response.

"It looks like it's murder, Justice. They found Ada Sinclair all right. They found her dead."

3

"Dead?" Ruff Justice repeated the word quietly. "What happened, Colonel?"

"I guess you'd know better than any of us, Ruff."

"How the hell would I know!"

"Don't use that tone with me, Justice," MacEnroe said stiffly.

"Why not? What are you going to do, sir? Lock me up? How long have you known me, Colonel? I've pulled a lot of stunts, maybe some of them unnecessary. But you know me well enough to know damn well I don't take young women out, force them to do evil things, and then kill them. You know it; Ray there knows it."

"We *don't* know it, Justice," the colonel said. "We weren't there. I have my duty—"

"Spare me the speech, will you?" The two men locked eyes for a minute. Justice asked, "Where did they find her? How was she killed?"

"Down near the river, Justice," MacEnroe said with some impatience, as if Justice already knew it all and was merely humoring him. "Half-dressed, butchered."

"Butchered," Justice repeated.

"Indian-style, but there's no wild Indians this near to Lincoln, and you know it as well as anyone. Maybe someone wanted to lay the blame on the Indians. Is that why you invented that story about the Cheyenne woman coming to your rescue?"

"Who found her?" Ruff asked.

"A search party under Sergeant Hart. She had been pretty well carved up with a knife. Fingers amputated, face disfigured. Never mind the rest of the details—you know how an Indian does his work."

"Yeah. Therefore I'm guilty."

"You were the last one to see her alive. You had an intimate relationship with her. Something—only you know what—very violent and deadly happened in that hotel room. Now Ada Sinclair is dead. She had your pistol with her. Wonder why you're accused of this, Justice?"

"That's right, I wonder," Justice said bitterly. "What happens now? You hang me?"

"After a trial, I expect so. You'll be transferred to Bismarck jail in the morning."

"Handing me over, are you? Washing your hands of me?"

"I do," the colonel said in a stony voice, "what has to be done, Justice." He turned to Albertson. "Let me out now, Sergeant. Unless you have something else to say, Justice."

"What do you want me to do? Confess?" Ruff asked cynically.

"Will you?"

"Sure. I confess to sleeping with the senator's daughter. If you believe the rest of it, to hell with you, Colonel MacEnroe."

The colonel started to step forward, but he caught himself. He turned sharply and marched from the cell, the door clanging shut behind him as Albertson closed and locked it.

Justice remained standing for a long while in the center of the cell as dusk faded to night beyond the tiny barred window. Then with a sudden, violent gesture he turned and returned to his bunk. He needed to sit for a while, to think, to brood. . . .

He had been asleep. The stars were bright in the window. The single blanket wasn't enough to keep him truly warm, and the sleep he needed hadn't come easily.

The tiny clinking sound had brought him instantly awake, instantly alert. Years on the plains caused him to reflexively reach for his holstered Colt .44 pistol, but now he had no gun belt. He was in the stockade at Fort Abraham Lincoln, Dakota Territory. Ada Sinclair had taken his gun and tried to shoot him with it. The pistol was evidence now, evidence in a murder trial that would provide a source of great entertainment for the local citizenry.

"They've been waiting to see me fall," Justice muttered to the night.

Then the memory of the small clinking sound came back, and he sat up. frowning. He looked toward the window, seeing nothing. Then his eyes searched the floor of his cell and he picked out the small iron object lying against the stone.

Ruff threw his blanket aside and rose, going to the object, eyes shuttling to the cell door and the corridor beyond, where a duty corporal stood watch.

He crouched, fingered the object, and then lifted the key closer to his eyes. Was it the right key? Where in hell had it come from?

"If it is"—and it had to be—"I've got at least one friend left in the world."

Ruff moved to the door on silent feet. Dim light from a lantern bled into the dark corridor. A low voice came from beyond the heavy oak door farther along. Ruff reached through the bars and inserted the key. It fit, but would it turn?

Slowly he turned it and the flanges caught tumblers.

The heavy lock clicked open and Justice tried the door. Open.

Justice removed the key, pocketed it, and stood watching, listening. There were at least two armed men beyond the heavy door. A man doesn't normally sit around talking to himself in the dead of night. Two soldiers were at least one too many. He waited.

After a time someone laughed and then the great iron-strapped outer door to the stockade fell shut. Silence.

Ruff waited, every small night sound alive in his ears. It was an hour later when the door to the corridor opened and a bored corporal entered to make his check.

He peered into each cell he passed, jingling his keys habitually, unconsciously. Passing Ruff's cell, he halted and tensed.

"Oh, Mister Justice!" The corporal breathed a sigh of relief. "Can't sleep?"

"Could you?" Ruff asked with a disarming smile.

"No, I guess not."

"Any chance of getting some coffee?" Ruff asked, hanging on to the door, his head against the bars.

"No, sir. Sorry. They don't allow that. Albertson would skin me alive."

"A chance for an escape, maybe?" Ruff asked.

"Yes. I suppose so."

"You don't have to worry much about me . . ." Justice suddenly swung the heavy iron door outward, and the corporal, leaning forward, took the edge of it on the skull. He sighed and fell back against the wall. Justice was out in seconds, snatching the key ring from his waist, dragging the corporal into the cell and locking him in.

Justice wiped back his long hair, looked up and down the corridor, and then moved on cat's feet to the oak door. Peering out, he saw no one. A pipe still burning, a mug of coffee, an open copy of the *Police Gazette*.

Ruff crossed the room, taking a shotgun from the wall

rack. At the outer door he paused. Footsteps, slow and heavy, approached him.

He pressed himself against the wall behind the door and waited. The door was unlocked and opened, and a soldier with a rifle in one hand, a cup of coffee in the other, stepped through.

"Cartwright?" he called, and Justice slammed the butt of the shotgun against the side of his skull. The rifle and tin cup clattered to the floor.

Working quickly, Justice dragged the soldier inside, closed the door, and stripped the man of his belt gun, cap, and tunic. Ruff pulled on the too-small tunic, adjusted the cap, and stepped out into the night.

He shouldered the shotgun he still carried, and crossed the space between the stockade proper and the surrounding fence. A lone guard walked his rounds to Ruff's right. The guard lifted a silent hand and Ruff raised his in return.

There was a judas gate to the left of the main gate to the stockade, and Justice slipped through. He stood for a minute in the shadows cast by the palings, studying the interior of the fort.

Lights glowed in the enlisted men's barracks and in the officers' quarters across the parade ground. In front of the sutler's store a group of enlisted men stood drinking bottled beer, arguing about something inconsequential and mysterious.

Ruff slid along the wooden wall toward the stables and the paddock beyond. Ducking under a corral rail, he moved to a wide-eyed stocky bay horse and took its mane, stroking its neck and speaking gently.

He led the horse silently toward the western gate, hearing a distant burst of laughter from the sutler's.

"Slipping out?"

A private appeared from the shadows, a grin on his face. He still wasn't near enough to recognize Justice. All he saw was the soldier's tunic, the cap.

"Yeah," Justice said sheepishly.

The soldier came closer. "Got something good in town?"

Ruff answered, "Yes, and no pass."

"Can't let you go out, soldier," the guard said, and then, coming a step nearer, he recognized Justice. "Mister—"

Ruff kicked him on the knee, and as the soldier crumpled up, with pain. Justice kicked him again, in the face.

"Sorry, friend," Ruff said, bending to pick up the guard's rifle, which he flung away.

Then he led the unsaddled horse to the gate, swung it open, and passed through, riding out onto the night-darkened prairie beyond Lincoln.

Behind Justice lights twinkled in Bismarck. Lincoln was still alive with sound and light, but he was free, riding into the night, which swallowed him up. He urged the bay horse on, running it for two miles before he slowed the animal and finally halted it—where? Where was he going? What in hell could he do to clear his name, if anything?

There were the far mountains and the Crow Indians who would welcome him home—home where he had lived for almost two years. But he would still be a hunted man, a man with a shadow over him.

The bay blew and Ruff stroked its neck, anger slowly building within him. Someone had framed him, someone wanted him dead. Someone had killed the senator's daughter.

They weren't going to get away with it, no matter who they were. Maybe the colonel hadn't seen it, but Justice knew something was going on here, something deeper than any of them suspected.

"They won't get away with it," he promised the night and the uncaring horse. Maybe they wanted him to run—*who?* He wasn't going to do it; he knew it already. Someone had a price to pay and there was only Justice to see that it was paid.

What about the Cheyenne woman? Justice asked himself. Where had she come from? What had she wanted? It seemed like a dream, that night with her. But an Indian, or someone who knew their ways, had killed the senator's daughter. Why not the Cheyenne woman?

"But why?"

The night had no answers, nor did the stolen bay horse, now heated and impatient. Ruff moved on, taking pains to cover his tracks, walking the bay through rocky country and up a narrow stream. Finding a second stream, he crossed it, backed the horse after reaching broken ground, reentered the stream, and rode *down*stream.

A good Indian tracker could follow Ruff's sign, but he would have to be very good, and it would take time. Justice was also counting on the fact that Lincoln's Indian scouts were closer to him than to the uniformed officers. Shay and Takim, both Delaware scouts, used all of their skills to track renegade Cheyenne or Sioux war parties. Maybe they wouldn't show quite as much conscientiousness in following their friend, who had, after all, done nothing but kill his white woman.

Maybe. At any rate Justice had a good lead for the time being. Free of the stream again, he lined out across the plains, using speed instead of wile to separate himself from any pursuit.

Just then he needed a place to think things out, to plan a course of action. There had to be some clue as to what was going on. Ada Sinclair hadn't singled him out to kill for no reason at all. The Cheyenne girl hadn't appeared for no reason. Just now Ruff couldn't get a handle on any of it, but soon he would.

He would, and when he had it, someone would find the scout down their throat.

He rode on through the night across the dark plains, the

rising half-moon lighting his way toward Carrizo Gorge. He had a friend there—if the renegades had let him stay—and Abel Pettigrew wasn't the sort to let Justice down, to back away from trouble, to let his lip slip at the wrong time.

Pettigrew was one of the old breed, there on the plains before the army, before the towns and their so-called civilization. He knew the Indians, had built an uneasy truce with them, a truce built on mutual respect. They had taken Abel Pettigrew once, taken him and scarred him and lopped off his left hand. They had left Pettigrew for dead, but the plainsman had started a fire, cauterized the stump of his hand, and risen to his feet to go after the Indians who had done it. He had found them in a night camp and killed all of them—all but one. In the manner of the Indians themselves he had let one brave live to return to the home camp with news of the deaths, to carry the legend of the one-handed white to the Cheyenne.

The sun was rising, trickling color against a gray-washed Dakota sky when Ruff Justice found the little sod-roofed cabin tucked up against the cedar-studded bench along the Arrowhead River.

The bay moved slowly, weary from the night's work. Its hooves brushed the morning frost from the long grass as Justice approached the cabin, noticing the low profile of the featureless house. The slot windows were useful for firing rifles, useless for letting sunlight into the house. But then Pettigrew wasn't in the house much during daylight hours—he was out working, trying to hold on to what he had. He managed to scrape a living from the hard land, trapping, tending his small vegetable patch, watching the sheep he had brought up from Colorado, mustanging from the wild herds in the hills beyond, fishing, cutting wood. Whatever it took, Pettigrew did, and he did it with one good hand.

The front door of the shack opened as Justice rode

toward the house where full grown cottonwoods stood bunched together, dark against the new dawn. A hog rooting happily in the dark Dakota earth grunted challengingly and then waddled away from the approaching horse.

"Justice?" The man in the doorway held a rifle. He peered out at the incoming rider and then grinned, coming forward, his gait uneven—the Cheyenne had once put an arrow into his right leg. "Damn all, it is you, you long-haired rascal!"

" 'Morning, Abel," Justice said, swinging down from the bay. "Hope I didn't disturb your slumbers."

"Slumbers, damn you." Pettigrew grinned. "I been up since first light splittin' wood, and you know it."

Pettigrew placed his rifle under his left arm and embraced Justice with the right. He looked at the army cap, the tunic Justice wore, at the unsaddled army bay, and asked, "Been in an Indian fight, Ruffin?"

"Something like that."

"You come in and set and tell me about it. Army around, is it?" Pettigrew asked, leading Justice into his house, arm still over Ruff's shoulders.

"Not that I know of," Justice replied. "And I hope they aren't."

Pettigrew frowned. He was of medium stature with one constantly squinting eye. His gray whiskers never seemed to be more than an inch long, never seemed to be shaved. His eyes were alive with amusement and a knowledge of the world that no man has who hasn't walked close to death.

"Odd thing for you to say, Ruffin. Sit yourself to the table and I'll pour coffee. What's happened, son?"

"Nothing much." Ruff took off the army cap and sat to the crude puncheon table. "Colonel MacEnroe wants to hang me."

"When don't he?" Pettigrew chuckled.

"I'm afraid he's serious this time, Abel."

"Oh?" The older man brought two cups of coffee to the table and sat opposite Justice. The front door stood open and the brilliantly colored dawn illuminated the room. "What's happened, Ruffin? Need a friend?"

"Yes, Abel, I do." Ruff sipped his coffee. "They want me for murder, for killing a senator's daughter. Senator Cotton Sinclair."

"Bullshit," Abel said with much conviction.

"That's what it is." Ruff took a sip of the strong dark coffee and shed the army tunic he had borrowed.

"Colonel MacEnroe would know that ain't true. You kill a woman?" Abel Pettigrew chuckled. "You might do about anything else with one, from what I've heard, but kill a useful female? Never!" Another thought burrowed its way into Pettigrew's mind. "Cotton Sinclair, ain't he the one come out here to see what the Indian situation is in Dakota?"

"He's the one," Ruff answered.

"Thought so. I got me a Philadelphia paper only three weeks old. Read that from hello to good-bye, corset ads included. There was a write-up and a lot of editorial railing."

"What sort of railing?" Justice asked.

"Said we didn't need no senator to come out and see what the situation was. The Indians needed killing and that was that. Stupid bastard!" Pettigrew said with disgust.

"Back East," Justice said, "they wouldn't understand that attitude—from a man the Indians've treated like they have you."

"No, Ruffin, I guess they wouldn't. The way I figure it is that I've got the right to come here and live. The Indians got the right to try to chase me out if they don't like it. Well, they tried and I didn't go; now everyone pretty much agrees I got the right to stay. And I still figure the Cheyenne got the right to what they've got. Fair's fair."

"Where's Sinclair stand exactly, according to that Philadelphia paper?"

"Apparently a little too much on the Indians' side to suit some. Mostly he just wants to know what is happening out here, if we can work out a peace. I never figured out why we couldn't myself. Ask the Indians for a part of it, pay 'em fair, and use it."

"Maybe we ought to send you to Congress," Ruff teased.

"Me, with those crawfishers and charlatans and easy-chair boys!" Pettigrew was incensed. "I'll say one thing, Ruffin T. Justice, I've a little too damned much integrity for that kind of position. Beg pardon for tooting my own horn, but my ma taught me never to lie, to respect the laws of the land. No, Congress wouldn't suit me at all. I'm for the open land and living my own life. All I want Congress to do is leave me the hell alone. 'Course, they can't. It's against their grain."

Ruff got back to the main subject. "Senator Sinclair must have some powerful enemies."

"He's got 'em, all right. A lot of people—developers, railroad people, goldrushers, say move the Indians out now, by any means available. They're no damned good. Varmints and nothing else. Push 'em out and let civilization come through. Make way for the iron horse and the plow."

"I wonder if any of them would kill his daughter for revenge."

"I don't know. Makes no sense, Ruffin."

"Whoever did it tried to make it seem like Indians had done it—except MacEnroe and Sinclair decided it was me."

Pettigrew rubbed his whiskers meditatively. "Maybe," was all he said in reply.

"That's it—maybe. I don't know enough about the situation to understand what's going on. I don't suppose you've still got that newspaper, Abel."

"Sure I've got it—kept it for the illustrated corset ads. Want to have a look?"

"If you don't mind. There's a lot I don't know about Washington politics. Maybe it would help me to learn something."

"Can't see how, but you're welcome. Meanwhile I'll do something a little more practical for you." He nodded toward the open door. "You partial to that army bay, Justice?"

"Not at all."

"Then I'll get rid of it. Trade you a piebald gelding I've got, a good horse."

"That sticks you with the army bay," Ruff objected.

"Don't worry about that. I've got ways of getting rid of it. Trade him to the Cheyenne; they like a big horse when they can come by one. I'll bring home three or four mustangs in trade. Then," Abel said, rising and walking to a corner bureau, "I'll bury that army gear you were wearing." He slapped a torn newspaper on the table, saying, "Here's that business about Sinclair, Justice. Take it, read it, and I hope to hell you can find something in there that'll keep you from hanging."

4

Justice read the paper from one side to the other, skipping the well-perused corset ads, and when he was through, he had more knowledge of Cotton Sinclair's congressional battles, but he hadn't learned a single specific thing that might help him.

A group of congressmen, persuaded by various lobbyists, had apparently challenged Sinclair to produce a document on why the Indians shouldn't be punished and exterminated, especially in the wake of the Custer debacle, which still rubbed most Americans the wrong way. Cotton Sinclair had risen in the Senate and vowed to do just that: to bring back a fair and unbiased report on the state of the West and the progress of its war against the plains tribes.

With a lot of hoopla—mocked by the Philadelphia paper—Sinclair had started west with his beautiful young daughter, the first leg of the journey planned from Washington to Pittsburgh via railroad. There the factual account of things ended and the ranting of some unknown Pennsylvania editor had begun.

Abel Pettigrew returned just as Ruff was finishing the article. "Got that stuff buried in the garden."

"Thanks, Abel."

"For nothing. I took that bay up where no one's going

to find it. and brought the piebald around. I'd appreciate it if you can bring him back sometime. He's a good horse."

"I'll see that he gets back, Abel," Ruff promised.

The older man nodded at the paper. "Got through all that, did you?"

"I did. Makes you wonder what they have against Cotton Sinclair, doesn't it?"

"Nothin', I figure. They just want a little war out here to fill up their newspapers. Lucky if they don't get it."

"Why's that? Has there been trouble out this way?" Justice wanted to know.

"Trouble, in spades. Fist is raising hell."

"That doesn't sound like Fist." The Cheyenne war leader had been one of the leading troublemakers up along the border, but the word was that he had had a dream of peace. At any rate he hadn't given the army trouble for well over a year. He was one of the renegade leaders Sinclair had hoped to meet with, according to that newspaper article.

"He burned out the Watkins family upriver, hit a wagon train on the Oregon Fork."

Ruff frowned. "Does the army know about this?"

"They will. Happened day before yesterday. Len Watkins was the only massacre survivor—he was riding south toward Lincoln. Me, I've been bringing more stores in the house, keeping all three rifles ready."

"Would Fist try you, Abel?"

"Hell, I've lived among the Indians for seventeen years, Ruffin, and I still don't know what they're going to do from one minute to the next. I just try to be careful."

"That's all a man can do," Justice said, yawning as he spoke.

"You won't make it far without some rest, Ruffin."

"I'll find me a place," the scout answered. "Don't want to linger here too long. Likely the marshal is on my trail by now—with a U.S. senator involved, McCracken won't just sit on his hands."

"Bob McCracken? Don't tell me he's marshal now?"

"He is. Good choice, huh?" Ruff said dryly.

"Well, he was a good drinking friend to a lot of people. Maybe that qualified him."

"It seems to be all it takes in a lot of places," Justice answered, and he yawned again.

"Look, Ruffin, you see that cot—you sack out there for a time. No sense you going up into the hills. I'll set watch for you."

"Might mean trouble, Abel."

"Ruffin, all my life's been trouble. Don't worry. If it's McCracken, he'll spend half the day making sure he's got a great whoppin' posse to bring along for protection. And he'll sure as hell never track you if you're as good as ever."

Ruff was too tired to argue. He simply thanked Abel again, walked to the cot, and rolled up, falling asleep immediately.

By the sun three or four hours had passed when Abel shook him. "Didn't figure you wanted to sleep too long," Pettigrew said.

"No, that's all right."

"Besides, you got someone on your trail."

Ruff's eyes narrowed. He sat up quickly and peered at Pettigrew. "Army?"

"No."

"McCracken, then?" Justice said.

"No, not him. Maybe a scout for one or the other. Lone man out there. Just made him out once from the roof. Holding back a mile or so down in a coulee."

"Shay maybe, or Takim." Justice wondered if he had overestimated the loyalty Lincoln's two Indian scouts had to him, underestimated their devotion to duty.

"Maybe nobody," Pettigrew said, "maybe one of

Fist's warriors having a look at my place. But the way he's holding back makes me think he's on your tail, Justice."

"All right. Thanks, Abel. I'll get going then." Ruff stood and walked to the door, running a hand across his dark hair. He looked out one of the cabin's slit windows but could see little on the sun-bright plains outside.

"Want me to hold him back, Justice?" Pettigrew lifted his rifle meaningfully.

"No. We don't know who it is. It might mean trouble for you. If you shot Shay or some scout the marshal has picked up, they'd have you down in Bismarck trying a rope necktie on."

"Whatever you say, Ruffin. While you were asleep, I moved that piebald horse. He's in the cottonwoods near the river. Figured you could slip out the back and move out through the trees."

"Thanks, Abel." Ruff clapped the frontiersman on the shoulder. "I guess this means I owe you one."

"Sure it does—and I know you'll pay me back if I need a favor. Folks know you, Ruffin; folks know your word is good, that you'll be there if they need help. What bothers me," Pettigrew muttered, "is why Colonel MacEnroe don't realize you couldn't have done this thing they're accusing you of. If anyone should know you, it's him."

Justice had no answer for that one. It was something that bothered him too. He could understand Sinclair being distraught, angry, vengeful, but the colonel had let him down. It stung, and even if Justice got out of this, he wondered if things would ever be the same, if he could possibly work for the army again.

"Here." Pettigrew shoved a sack of supplies at Justice. "It ain't much. Coffee, salt, cornmeal."

"I appreciate it, Abel."

"You partial to that scattergun you're carrying, Ruffin?"

"Not particularly. It just sort of came to hand."

"That's what I thought. I got three rifles, Ruffin. I could trade you a Winchester for the shotgun. Lot of ducks down on the Arrowhead just now and I could use a good ten-gauge."

"That suits me, Abel—don't hurt yourself."

"Said I needed a shotgun, didn't I? Here." Abel took the rifle from under his left arm and thrust it at Justice. "There's cartridges in the sack there. You get going now, Justice. Get going, and good luck—watch your butt, though. Fist is out there."

"I'll watch it. Thanks again, Abel."

And with that Justice was gone, out the barred back door of the soddy and into the trees, moving swiftly toward the river. He found the saddled piebald gelding standing there, a deep-chested well-set-up horse with one white ear, one black. The rest of its blotched body was sleek and glossy. It cast an uncaring eye at Justice, patiently let the man tie on the sack of supplies and swing aboard. With utter indifference, the horse started forward briskly at the touch of Ruff's heels.

Justice splashed across the Arrowhead, which ran wide and shallow here. A dozen pintail ducks rose from an oxbow and circled. The sunlight dappled the earth beneath the trees and silvered the river.

Justice climbed the bluffs beyond, stopped the piebald on a narrow ledge, and swung down, looking back.

Someone was there, Abel had said, but Justice couldn't pick him out just then. He crouched and waited, tugging his hat down, Winchester across his knees.

The sun beamed down, cold and bright. A pair of crows swung past, cawing raucously. The wind worked in the cedars on the higher slopes, making mournful sounds. Still Justice waited; still he saw no one on his back trail. Abel came out once, took in an armload of wood, and returned to his cabin. The river flowed past silently. Nothing. No one moved on the plains. Whoever it was back there had either given up or was very patient.

Two hours on, Justice saw the riders coming. There had to be twenty of them, kicking up dust that plumed hundreds of feet into the air and stretched out a quarter of a mile behind them.

McCracken and his posse.

Justice stood, holding his horse's reins. He waited until he was sure it was Marshal McCracken—the big, barrel-chested man with the red vest was hard to miss—and then he led the horse up into the cedars, swung aboard, and rode on.

Where was he headed? Justice had become a man on the run. His original idea had been to clear up this false murder charge somehow and make sure that the real murderer was punished; yet every mile he rode from Lincoln and Bismarck made that chance slimmer.

He could have doubled back, but at that moment he didn't even have an idea of where to look, of who might have murdered Ada Sinclair. Unless it was that Cheyenne woman—that dream thing, that needful, trigger-happy Indian girl.

"And just where in hell would I find her?"

Had she even been real? Ruff was riding through a murky nightmare world where nothing seemed solid, substantial.

Ruff rode the long wooded bluff until it broke off into a series of ragged, time-eroded hills that funneled down toward a grassy valley beyond.

It had been a pretty place, long silver-green grass flooded with black-eyed Susans, dotted with lupine and daisies. Now the grass was black, the flowers gone. The house that had been built beside the hidden rocky springs was charred and desolate.

There wasn't much left of the Watkins place, not much left of a simple dream of a few acres, a warm house, a family to live with.

Justice had visited the house before, when George Watkins was alive, when his small, cheerful wife had baked biscuits and served them with home-smoked ham to any guest and to the large, happy family.

Fist. What had turned Fist into a raider again? The man had been wild as a younger warrior, eager to establish his reputation, to spill white blood. But now it was said he had dreamed of peace. Had another dream come to wash away that one?

Justice walked the piebald horse across the burned grass to the empty house. Beneath the oaks, scorched and blackened themselves by warfire, five new graves rested. Len Watkins had taken the time to do that mournful job.

Justice swung down, letting the horse water at the seep from the springs above the house. He stood at the gravesite for a moment and then, shaking his head, turned away. This would do no good for the Cheyenne. Sinclair, already in a savage mood, would report this to his congressional committee and the wars would begin again—the renegade had chosen the wrong time to begin his holy war anew.

Justice walked the yard, going to the burned-out house. The earth outside was littered with cartridges. Their spent bullets had riddled the house, striking flesh, innocent flesh, that of women and children.

Justice idly picked one up, wiping the ash from the shiny brass. They were .44-40s. The Indians had repeating rifles then, and plenty of them. Something tugged at the back of Ruff's consciousness and fell away again before he could grasp it.

Something was wrong.

His subconscious flashed that message to the center of his reasoning mind, but before he could lock onto it and chew at the thought, the guns opened up from the hills.

Ruff threw himself to the ground and rolled toward the corner of the burned house, taking shelter behind the stone foundation. Bullets rang off the stone, scattering rock dust.

"Underestimated him, dammit all," Justice said half-aloud.

McCracken was there. From the hill slopes a dozen guns had begun to fire, and Justice was pinned down. There was no way out, no way but the dark chute leading to the gates of hell.

The marshal and his deputies worked their way down the wooded hills, firing as they came; and Justice, his head low, unfired rifle in his hands, did not answer their shots. He could have taken a man or two out, someone he knew from Bismarck, a storekeeper or adventure seeker, some honest citizen trying to track down a woman killer, but in the end they would take him—take him dead.

Justice wanted to live. It wasn't fear that caused him to make that decision, but the sudden knowledge that he *knew* what was wrong with all of this, knew what was swirling around all the innocent people of the territory, bringing death.

"All right," Ruff Justice shouted above the guns. "I give up!" He hurled his Winchester out into the open.

There was a moment while the guns sputtered to a disbelieving halt before a voice answered. "Justice?"

"It's me, McCracken."

Another pause followed. Maybe they couldn't believe that Ruff Justice, scout, rough country explorer, gunman, would surrender so easily. They had made up their minds that they would have to kill him before retaking him, perhaps.

"All right." It was McCracken who responded. "You got a belt gun, Justice? Throw it out too."

Ruff unbuckled his stolen army revolver and flung it out onto the burned grass before the burned Watkins house.

"Stand up," the marshal of Bismarck said, and there was surprise in his voice, surprise and elation. McCracken was a town marshal without much background. Bringing in Ruff Justice alive was something sure to solidify his political standing.

Justice stood and raised his hands, walking forward as the barrel-chested marshal and his posse emerged from the trees and advanced slowly on the burned-out Watkins farmhouse.

The man in the lead was a barfly named Jack Crandall. He was blond, young, and considered himself tough. Puffing, McCracken caught up as Crandall and another man took Justice by the arms.

"Got the son of a bitch," Crandall said loudly, gleefully. He decided to celebrate by throwing a fist into Ruff's belly. Justice was slammed back, the wind knocked out of him as Crandall, tossing his rifle to a friend, came in to do it again.

Justice kicked him in the face and Crandall grabbed at his broken nose, howling with pain. The man on Ruff's other side tried to hammer his skull with a pistol barrel, but Justice gave him an elbow in the eye, hard. The man staggered back cursing and screaming. Justice stood still, waiting for McCracken.

"You're under arrest, Ruff Justice," McCracken said loud enough for the people back in Bismarck to hear.

"I guess I am," was Ruff's response.

Jack Crandall, his face smeared with blood, was pawing his way through the gathered deputies toward Justice. "Let me have him," Crandall yelled, "just let me get my hands on him!"

McCracken showed that he wasn't entirely stupid. "Back off, Jack. We've got him. You and Shaughnessy deserved what you got."

Crandall didn't like it, but he stopped and was held back by a few good men in the posse, like Art Paulsen, who had hunted with Justice and had once been in an Indian fight with him.

"Good work, Marshal," someone said, and McCracken beamed.

"That takes care of one of 'em," the marshal said, "and maybe, by God, *both* of 'em."

Ruff's eyes lifted to the marshal's face. Now, what in hell did *that* mean? Were they looking for someone else as well? Before Justice could ask a question, a tall man in a town suit, white hat, sporting new boots and a brand-new Remington revolver, stepped forward and shook McCracken's hand.

He was slender and green-eyed, wearing a thin mustache. "It's good to know there's one white man in this territory that knows what he's up to," the tall man said.

"Why, thanks, Mister Todd," McCracken said. He tugged at his own red vest and beamed some more, maybe smelling reelection.

They must have passed Len Watkins on the trail, for they all seemed to know what had happened to the farm. Todd, the tall man with the new gear, said, "Look what the bastards get away with—what the hell's wrong with the army out here? Four graves."

"Let 'em try us," someone very young and very ignorant said. "Just let Fist try his hand with us."

McCracken suddenly looked more nervous than proud. He too surveyed the burned-out house and the graves. "Let's pull out," he said quietly. He repeated himself with more vigor. "Let's get out of here, men. We didn't come to fight Indians."

"Neither did the army," Todd said, and there was scattered laughter from the posse.

"And," the marshal said to Justice, "don't think I don't know that piebald horse, Justice. Maybe I'll just stop and pick up Abel Pettigrew for aiding and abetting."

"I stole the horse," Justice said.

"And you admit it! Good," McCracken said to an

appreciative audience. "Now we've got two charges to hang the bastard on."

"That," Todd said, looking into Ruff's eyes with a malevolence Justice couldn't figure, "is exactly what must be done. What will be done. Hang Ruff Justice. Hang him by the neck until he's dead."

5

Night camp was three miles south of the Arrowhead in a deep coulee where willows and a few cottonwoods struggled for life. The stars were bright, the red flames of the campfire low, the wind howling and cold. Guards walked the rim of the coulee, eyes alert for Fist and his raiders. Ruff Justice, hands tied behind him, sat watching the celebrating posse as they drank coffee and whiskey, smoked cigars, and magnified their own parts in the taking of the famous woman-killer Ruffin Tecumseh Justice.

"Coffee, Ruffin?"

Justice looked up to see Art Paulsen standing over him, two tin cups of coffee in hand.

"Hard to drink it this way, Art." Ruff grinned.

"I'll untie you if you won't come at my throat."

"McCracken might not like it."

"Screw McCracken. He's half-stewed anyway." Paulsen hesitated, though. "Your word, Justice?"

"You got it, Art."

Paulsen put the coffee down on a rock and untied the rope at Ruff's wrists. Justice brought his hands before him and rubbed them for a while before wrapping them around the tin cup Art handed him.

Paulsen squatted there, silently drinking his own coffee.

Justice asked, "What brought you along on this skunk hunt, Art?"

Paulsen shrugged. "Some of us wanted to see you weren't lynched out here, that's all. There was talk of making sure you never saw Bismarck again."

"Talk from who? Jack Crandall?"

"Him. And this Jesse Todd."

Jesse Todd. Why did that name ring a bell in Ruff's mind? He was sure he had never seen the man before. "Who is he anyway, Art?"

"Some dude. Politician or something from back East," Art said indifferently.

Then it came to Justice. "Sure, Jesse Todd." Todd had been mentioned in one of the Philadelphia paper's articles. He was an agent, a lobbyist for some development company that wanted to carve the plains into eighty-acre homesteads, to create homes for "good, decent Americans" and drive off the "butchering savages like Fist." Another door opened in Justice's mind and he sat staring toward the fire where Todd had seated himself next to McCracken.

"You know him, then?" Art asked.

"Not exactly, but Senator Cotton Sinclair does, I'll bet."

"I don't follow you."

"Never mind. Art, back at the Watkins place McCracken said something that puzzled me. He said he had *one* of them now and maybe *both* of them. What in hell was he talking about?"

"You don't know?"

"If I did, I wouldn't ask, Art."

Art Paulsen's honest, narrow face puckered up a little. "He meant he had the man who killed Ada Sinclair. That's one. We had another little mystery in Bismarck maybe you didn't hear about. A girl from the Sternwheeler has turned up missing."

"Which one?" Justice frowned. He wasn't a saloongoer but he knew most of the girls.

"Becky Tandy. Know her?" Art asked.

"I'm not sure. Was she a blonde?"

Art nodded. "That's right."

"In her early twenties. Fairly tall, say five-foot-five," Justice said.

"That's right. You did know her then?"

"No, Art, I didn't. I never saw this Becky Tandy in my life."

"Then . . ." Art didn't finish his question. Crandall, carrying a rifle, had come to where he sat with Justice. The bulky blond man's nose had swollen up to twice its size. When he spoke, it was as if it hurt him to do so.

"The marshal says to tie him up again. *Now*."

"All right," Art said agreeably. He was still watching Justice, wondering what was in the scout's mind. He rose to tie Justice's hands, but Crandall interfered.

"I'll do it, Art. You're too damned chummy with him. Hold my rifle."

Crandall walked to Justice, waiting for, hoping for trouble. But Ruff simply put his hands behind his back and waited as Crandall wrapped his wrists with savage tightness, grunting as he worked. Finished, he straightened up and studied Justice with satisfaction, taking his rifle from Art Paulsen.

"He won't get out of those, I'll promise you that."

Paulsen said nothing. He glanced again at Justice and then walked away, leaving Crandall to stand above Ruff.

"It'll be a pleasure to watch you learn to neck dance, Justice," Crandall hissed. "I'll be there with a picnic basket, and I'll be laughing when they spring the trap on you."

Justice kept his mouth shut. Crandall was waiting for an excuse, any excuse, to kick him or slap that gun barrel against his head. After a long minute's wait Crandall backed away, a small, animal hiss coming from his lips.

Justice watched him until he had returned to the fire to sit with Jesse Todd and the marshal. Then, with the wind rushing coldly through the coulee, Justice curled up to sleep the best way he could. Half-resolved thoughts were swimming through his mind, conjuring up dark and bloody images.

He woke suddenly. One eye opened to peer out at the cold night. The stars shined dully in a frosty sky. The moon was gone, the fire out, and someone was beside him. Someone who slipped a sharp knife between his wrists and slit the bonds that held them. Not far away, a guard lay unconscious against the dark earth.

Ruff rolled slowly to see the Cheyenne woman standing over him in the darkness. She beckoned with one finger, and Ruff rose silently to move off in a crouch through the willows, glancing back at the sleeping, cold camp.

They worked their way a quarter of a mile up the coulee and then climbed its sandy bank, the Cheyenne woman moving swiftly ahead of Justice. At the rim of the coulee she paused, waiting.

Ruff had asked her no questions, hadn't spoken. She had come to give him back his life. She had saved it once before and he trusted her.

Like players in a dream they crossed the starlit plains to a stand of mature oaks where two paint ponies stood waiting. The girl swung aboard one of the horses, tossed Ruff Justice a repeating rifle, and started off northward.

Justice was on the other horse's back, following her within seconds. A mile on, he caught up with her, took the bridle of her pony, and halted it.

"What, now, man of legend?" she asked.

"It is you, then?" Justice said, studying her face by starlight.

"It is me."

"You want to tell me what's going on. Who are you, anyway?"

"Spring Walker," she answered. "And you are Ruff Justice. Let us ride now."

"Ride where?" Justice asked, keeping hold of her pony's bridle.

"To see Fist, of course," she answered with honest surprise. Lovely and starlit, her face was very young, her deep eyes wide and bright.

"Fist." Justice repeated in a flat tone. "Why would I want to see Fist, Spring Walker?"

"Because he wishes to see you," she responded with a small shrug.

"Sorry, that's not quite enough reason," Justice said. "Fist has himself a war to make and I don't care to be around while he does it."

"Fist wants you," the girl said slowly as if talking to a child. "You must come."

"No."

"What will you do, then, go and be hung?"

"Spring Walker, what does Fist want me for? Fist doesn't like me at all. Once we met in a skirmish. He knew who I was. He shouted insults across the battlefield."

"Fist does not like you, no, but Fist trusts you."

"He does, does he?" Ruff said. "Sorry, I still don't want to see Fist. I've other things on my mind."

"But you must," she said calmly, "you *will*."

"You forget, Spring Walker, I'm the one with the rifle now," Justice said.

"Yes. You have the rifle," she agreed with some disappointment, "but you will find you do not have enough bullets to kill all of them."

"To kill . . ."

It was only then that Justice was aware of the Indians who had drifted out of the night prairie to flank them.

There were half a dozen armed Cheyenne warriors on either side, silent riders guiding them northward.

"And so it seems," Spring Walker said, a bright smile forming on her lovely face, "that you will see Fist."

"And so it seems," Ruff agreed grudgingly, "that I shall see Fist."

They rode silently on, through the broken hills, across empty prairie that was deep in frost, gleaming dully in the thin light of the stars and the pale rising moon.

It was dawn when they found the camp, hidden deep in the badlands. Set on a bluff sheltered by cedar and pine, by a rugged, serrated ridge, the Cheyenne camp contained a hundred people, perhaps more.

Ruff looked at his guide, nodded, and let himself be led on.

He would see Fist.

Fist, the warrior who hated him, who had threatened on that long-ago day to take Justice's long hair before he died . . . Fist, who had massacred the Watkins family and hit a settlers' wagon train only a few days ago.

The Cheyenne had never liked Ruff for a reason that was vague and nebulous to him. Even among the Sioux he had friends. Among the Cheyenne, none. Especially not Fist.

They had given him a rifle and it was loaded. They had not attempted to molest him. What did that mean? Nothing at all, but it gave Ruff a small hope that Fist actually did mean to *talk*.

"Are you frightened, man of legend?" Spring Walker asked.

"Damn right," Justice growled, and the smile that had been on her pretty lips burst into laughter.

They walked their horses down the dawn-colored slopes and into the camp, where smoke rose from cookfires into the hazy, reddening sky. Dogs emerged from their beds and began to yap at the incoming riders. Half-dressed warriors, with blankets across their shoulders and their hair loose, stood watching as Justice rode past them, Spring Walker behind and to his left on her paint pony.

The rest of the guard had fallen away and now there was only Justice and the Cheyenne girl as they rode to the great tepee ahead of them—the yellow one with the magic signs painted on its buffalo-hide walls.

They halted their horses and Justice glanced at his guide. Spring Walker nodded and he swung down, stretching his back as he gazed at the tepee. Its flap was closed.

Fist. Inside, the renegade sat and waited—and just what was on his mind?

Ruff didn't have to wait long to find out. The flap popped open and a stocky, scarred, bent-nosed Cheyenne came out. His black eyes took in Spring Walker and then Justice. He grunted with apparent satisfaction and said in the Cheyenne tongue, "Enter my lodge."

Fist reentered the tepee and Ruff followed, Spring Walker at his heels. There were warriors watching him—many warriors—and Ruff paused to leave the rifle, tilting it against the lodge before he ducked inside the stale, smoky home of the Cheyenne war leader.

"Sit," Fist said. "You are my guest, but forgive me if I do not follow etiquette with a white enemy."

Spring Walker translated this. Justice had some knowledge of the language, but apparently neither Indian felt it would be enough for him to follow whatever was to come.

Ruff sat crosslegged on a huge blue-and-brown blanket and waited, just waited as Fist stared at him, his hostile eyes searching and cold.

"You were a long time coming. Where have you been?" Fist asked. He could have been talking to either of them.

Spring Walker answered. "I went to get the man of legend, Fist. He was with the white woman with the yellow hair. I tried to kill her, but she ran." She hesitated then. "Before I could bring Ruff Justice, three soldiers came and took him away."

She had delicately omitted the interval of time between the two events, the time she had spent making love with Ruff Justice. She glanced at Ruff with a quick, pleading expression.

No, Fist wouldn't like it if he knew that the reason Spring Walker had failed to return was that she had been sleeping with her prisoner.

Spring Walker must have intended to bring Ruff out here all along, but Hardistein and his men had arrived unexpectedly and she had fled.

Ruff winked. He wasn't going to give her away.

"What happened? Why did the soldiers take you away?" Fist wanted to know.

"They thought I killed the other woman, the white woman."

"Did you?" Fist's eyes lighted with pleasure.

"No," Justice said, and the pleasure vanished from his black eyes.

Fist said something to Spring Walker Justice didn't catch. She didn't bother to translate it.

"Did they let you go?" Fist wanted to know.

"No, I escaped and rode north, but the marshal caught me. Then Spring Walker turned me loose."

"I see," Fist said with a deep frown. He was silent for a minute, then asked, "Do you know why you are here?"

"No."

"For the peace," Fist replied almost with impatience.

"For the peace. What peace, Fist?"

The Cheyenne said, "I dreamed of peace. I must make peace. Peace, or all of my people will die."

"You got a funny way of making peace," Ruff said,

recalling the Watkins family. Spring Walker looked at him with curiosity, but Justice just shook his head.

Fist went on, "We must have peace. But I must know what will happen to my people."

"Why ask me? Why not meet with Colonel MacEnroe?"

"I don't trust a soldier, no soldier," Fist said with a vehement hand gesture.

"Colonel MacEnroe is a good—"

"No soldier. Soldiers make war. I wish to make peace. I take no soldier's word for what will happen to me, to my people. I know only one white who keeps his word, one who kills when he has promised to kill, one who passes in peace when he promises to pass in peace. This man is one I despise. He is one I have often wanted to kill. This man is called Ruff Justice. It is him I wished to talk to."

"Me?" Justice said with a short laugh. "I'm no politician, no government agent."

"No. Why would I trust those people?" Fist said bitterly.

"It's a funny time to talk peace, Fist. The territory is up in arms just now. They want your scalp just as you've wanted mine."

"This I know," Fist said quietly. He was rubbing his wrist with his hand, looking tensely past Ruff toward some distant point. "They want to kill me. They want to kill all of my people."

"I'll ask you flat out: did you or one of your people kill a white woman and butcher her?"

"No!"

"A wagon trail at Oregon Fork—did you attack it?"

"No," Fist said even more sharply.

"The Watkins family. Did you massacre them?" Ruff demanded.

"No, no, no! I have a dream of peace. Why would I make

war? I did none of these things. My people did none of these things! It was someone else, Ruff Justice."

"Someone else? Who?"

"It was," Fist answered, "the Thunder Riders. It is they who have done these things, Ruff Justice. The Thunder Riders who do their murders on the plains."

6

"The Thunder Riders?" Ruff looked from Fist to Spring Walker, waiting for an explanation. "Who in hell are they?"

There was a long pause before Fist answered, "Whites, Ruff Justice. White men who ride the plains. Many whites."

"Whites?" Justice let that sink in. He considered the possibility that Fist was lying, but a look into those dark eyes convinced him that the Indian was speaking the truth as he knew it. "Why, Fist, why are they doing it?"

"I do not know."

"Whites killed the Watkins family, whites hit the Oregon Fork wagon train."

"Just so." Fist leaned closer. "And you must tell the army this—you must tell the people of the town on the Missouri that whites are killing and not Fist. You must tell them that Fist has dreamed of peace!"

"Yeah," Justice said. "That's a fine idea, but you're forgetting one thing, Fist. If I go back, they'll arrest me and hang me for murder."

"And if you do not go back, Ruff Justice, there will be a terrible war on the plains. A war that will soak the prairie with the blood of my people, with the blood of your people."

"Not only would they hang me, Fist, they wouldn't give me time to speak, wouldn't listen to anything I might be able to say," Justice pointed out. "They've already come to the conclusion that I'm a liar and a scoundrel."

Fist was silent for a moment, fingering a pipe with a red stone hatchet-head bowl. "Then, what use have I for you, Ruff Justice?" he asked at last.

"Not a lot."

"No. No use at all," the Cheyenne leader said. Anger and disappointment were mingled in his voice. "Go now, then. Go on your way—and ride far from this country, Justice. Far from it, for there will be more war, a great war fought to the last warrior. This I promise you."

Ruff started to say something else, but the black eyes of Fist repeated the command to go, and so with a nod he rose, stepped outside into the cold, clean air, picked up his rifle, and slid onto the pony's back.

The Cheyenne watched him go, their faces revealing nothing. They would die, all of them. A lot of settlers would die. Many soldiers and friends of Justice's, because of these so-called Thunder Riders. That was assuming Fist was telling the truth about them; Justice believed him.

He believed him because it fit in with what he already knew. This Jesse Todd had shown up from the East for no apparent reason, an agent for a land-development company and a lobbyist. Todd knew that Cotton Sinclair was coming to Dakota to look into the Indian situation, knew that if Sinclair found a peaceful resolution to things, his company was finished.

There were a lot of people who wanted the Indian wiped out. They just needed a little fuel for their warfires. Such as massacres on the plains, settlers killed, wagon trains attacked.

Nothing could be easier. Hire an army if you had to; it would be worth it to the land grabbers in the end. So what if a few sodbusters got killed? So what if a bunch of dirty Indians got blamed for it and the army had to move in?

Someone had known about Fist's intention of contacting the whites through Justice, and so Justice had to go.

"And that means the senator's daughter was working with them," Justice said aloud. "Why?" And why had they killed her? Maybe they hadn't killed her at all. Justice had been pondering that idea.

"Becky Tandy," he said to the Indian horse. The pony's ears twitched. Ruff had never met her, but she was a blonde about the same age and size as Ada Sinclair. The corpse the soldiers found had been mutilated—maybe to place the blame on the Cheyenne, maybe also so that no one would realize it wasn't Ada Sinclair at all but a kidnapped dance-hall girl who unluckily resembled the senator's daughter.

Try proving any of it. Try walking into the colonel's office and telling them what was going on.

"What, then?" Justice halted his horse in the pine woods above the deep red gorge, watching the slender, winding stream flow southward toward the long plains. The wind was very cold. A lone eagle drifted majestically on the wind currents above the gorge.

Spring Walker's pony made its slow way up the trail, and Justice waited for her, his face stern and set.

"What do you want?" he asked when she reached him.

"I will show you," she answered.

"Show me what?"

"I will show you where they are. I know in my heart what you will do, Ruff Justice. I know that you will seek the Thunder Riders and kill them all."

"You know that, do you?" Ruff grumbled. Yet the same idea had already been working in his mind. What else was there to do? Ride away from the whole damned mess and let the blood run? Not likely.

"Fist wants to kill them all, but he does not dare. They will find white bodies with arrows in them and then the Thunder Riders will have done what they were sent to do: begin a war. You," Spring Walker said ingenuously, "can kill them all because you are white."

"Fine," Justice answered. "I'll do that, then. Any idea *how?*"

Spring Walker said positively, "You will find a way, man of legend."

"Yeah." Ruff looked across the wide gorge, watching the eagle dip and soar. "I'll find a way." A way to get himself killed no matter which way he turned. If he went back to Lincoln, they'd string him up. If he tried to hide, sooner or later McCracken would find him. If he tried to do anything at all against these Thunder Riders, he would be chopped up into little pieces, the Cheyenne blamed, and hooray, another killer got what he deserved.

"It will rain," Spring Walker said.

Justice looked northward. The clouds were only a low dark band on the northern horizon, but maybe the girl was right. "It might," he said.

"Let us find shelter, then. Let us find shelter, Ruff Justice, and sleep for a little time—you and I. When the rain has passed, you will find your enemies and the enemies of the Cheyenne and you will kill them all. There is always time for death, let us make a little time for life."

Ruff was suddenly weary, weary with problems he couldn't solve and had no hope of solving, weary with the long riding. He looked at the bright-eyed Indian girl, thinking that perhaps her idea wasn't such a bad one. A little time for life.

"You know a place to shelter?" he asked her.

"I know a place," she assured him. "You will make love on me, then you will rest. When you awake, you will be ready to make war."

Justice didn't answer. It sounded good until she got to

the last part. Just how was he going to make war against an army? Spring Walker led the way through the pines, which swayed and groaned in the wind, and Justice fell in behind her, his little paint pony picking its way up the slope.

By the time they reached the crest, the clouds were much nearer, crowding the sky, towering and dark.

"There are caves farther along," Spring Walker said, and Justice looked downward to where the red gorge narrowed and jutted higher above the riverbed. He had heard that there were caves up along here somewhere, caves used by a people who lived here in a distant time, before the Sioux and the Cheyenne had come. He had never explored them—it hadn't seemed like much of an idea with Fist still holding the territory.

The girl worked her way surely northward and then found the narrow hidden trail she had been seeking. They rode across the face of the red bluff as the clouds storming in from the north began to drop scattered rain. The wind gusting up the gorge became a shrieking, malevolent thing.

The caves appeared around a bend in the narrow trail; honeycombing the cliff face, they stared out, hollow-eyed, at the storm and the river.

"Here," Spring Walker said. "There is room for the horses."

Her hair was pearled with raindrops, her dark eyes shining. It was growing colder and she was shivering a little as she slipped from her pony's back and led it forward into the hollow darkness of the cavern.

Ruff followed her, feeling the cold wind himself. Inside, it was dry, the wind absent, a prowling thing shut out by the cave. Still it hummed and whined and growled in the canyon below.

The girl crouched over her gathered fuel of packrats' nests, straw, and twigs, and fire sparked in the darkness. Her face was brightened by the growing flames. Spring Walker puffed gently on the flames and the fire grew, lighting the cave's interior. Outside, the rain began to fall in earnest, slanting down out of a cold sky. They could hear the river, distant and murmuring, and the crash of thunder.

"Soon it will be warm," the Cheyenne girl said. "Soon it will be good for making love."

Soon it was.

Ruff stripped off his buckskins and lay on a bed made of their blankets and discarded clothing. Above him, fire glossed and sleek, the Cheyenne woman stood, naked, hands on hips, her upthrust breasts proud and full, her lips parted with emotion.

Ruff was on his back, watching her as she approached, her hips swaying fluidly, her eyes alight with need and with the reflected glow of the firelight.

"No gun this time," Justice said.

"If I need one," she said, her eyes combing his hard, eager body, "I will get one."

Justice half-sat up, took her hand, and tugged her to him. "You don't need one," he promised, and she went down to him, meeting his lips with her own. Her hand ran across his chest and abdomen to his crotch, finding his solid erection, toying with it.

Spring Walker laughed with the pleasure she felt and tossed her loose hair back as she straddled Ruff, fitting herself to him. She allowed him to slide easily into her body as she swayed against him, hands on his hard stomach, the lightning outside the cave flashing warmly against the sky.

Ruff's hands cupped her breasts, his thumbs working across her erect nipples. Spring Walker nudged him with her pelvis. Then she began to batter him as her mouth fell open and the trickle of warmth within her became a gushing, open floodgate.

Ruff clenched her hard buttocks and drew her against

him. He lifted his head and bit at her nipples teasingly as she reached behind her, feeling his sack tight against her. She pitched and rolled and muttered words of delight in her own tongue, in no language, in the vague, heated words of love.

She collapsed against Ruff, her body warm against his, her breasts comforting, her lips teasing ear and throat and eyes as she fought against her own onrushing climax, losing the battle.

Spring Walker cried out with joy, bit at her knuckle to stifle the cry, and clung to Justice as he slowly, deliberately thrust against her, slowly and purposefully until his own need made his movements a wild plunging, a back-arching drive toward his sudden, loin-wrenching completion.

Slowly then they rocked against each other, touching, their lips brushing the other's body while the low fire crackled and the storm washed down. Finally they slept, Spring Walker covering Ruff's body with her own.

Justice slept and the storm outside raged. He slept and from out of his dreams the Thunder Riders came: faceless, dark, and bloody. Rain swirled around them and they carried severed Cheyenne heads. Behind them a blond woman in a wind-twisted white gown laughed and held up another bloody head: the head of Ruff Justice.

Ruff slept the day away and most of the night. When he awoke, it was to a rain-blurred dawn, a warm fire, and the soft kiss of an Indian woman who crouched beside him.

"Now you have made love, man of legend, now you have slept. Now you will rise and kill the enemies of the Cheyenne. Now you must destroy the Thunder Riders."

Justice didn't bother to answer. The world was insane, this Cheyenne woman was insane. If he had any sense, he'd ride out of the country, ride to San Francisco or farther, and let the insanity have its way on the plains. Except that meant that many would die horrible deaths. Many.

They rode out into the drizzle of dawn. The sky was alight with diffuse deep reds and oranges as sunrise tried to overpower the gloom of the day.

Northward they rode, up out of the long red gorge and into the timber once more, hardly speaking. They were two people riding toward Hades, futile and small and soulless.

It was noon under clearing skies before Spring Walker halted her pony and pointed down a grassy slope toward a distant, dark collection of tents and shacks thrown up alongside a shallow silver creek.

"There," she said in a voice so small and strangled that the single word came out as a gasp. "That is where they are."

The horse beneath Justice shifted its feet and blew. The cold wind drifted its mane. He sat the pony's back and looked toward the town, if that was what it could be called.

"Where in hell did they come from?" Justice wondered aloud. There had to be a hundred men in the camp, milling around, watering horses, gambling, or sleeping off liquor in their shacks and tents.

"They have been coming for a long time. Two of them, or six or ten together. Fist would have killed them, but he dreamed of peace. Later, he thought, the white authorities would tell these people to leave. These men who do not work, who do not hunt, but only," she said, "kill. These are the Thunder Riders, Ruff Justice."

"A hired army of scum collected from all over the West," Justice said quietly. "Come to fuse a war that'll leave a lot of people dead and a handful of men back East wealthy."

"You will not allow it," Spring Walker said.

Ruff sighed, bracing himself for a moment. "No," he responded, "I won't allow it." Somehow these people would be stopped—somehow, but he hadn't a clue how.

"Good!" Spring Walker brightened with the idea. "I will go down with you and watch you kill them all."

"You won't go anywhere with me," Justice said, restraining her as she started her pony forward. "What you'll do is go back to Fist's camp and stay there—and if you can, find a way to get Fist to drift your people out of this area, maybe toward the Canadian border."

"Fist will never leave!"

"Then he'll continue to get blamed for all of this."

"No," Spring Walker said with confidence, "because you will fix it all, Ruff Justice."

"Sure I will," Justice said ironically. Then he took the girl by the shoulders and dragged her face to his. He kissed her lips deeply before he ordered, "Get out of here now. Ride home. I've got things to do, woman."

She watched him silently, her dark hair lifted by the wind. Then, without a word, she turned her pony upslope, leaving Ruff Justice alone to sit and watch the dirty little encampment. With a slow, vivid curse, he heeled his pony and started downward toward the Thunder Riders' shack town.

7

Justice's heart raced in his chest and swelled into his throat as he rode into the town of killers. His hand gripped the Winchester; he carried the rifle so tightly that it was cramped and sweaty, despite the coolness of the day. Ruff half-expected a bullet in the back with each step the plodding Indian pony took. Although interested eyes lifted toward him as he passed the torn, patched former army tents and ramshackle buildings, no one so much as called out a challenge.

These men had been gathered from far and wide. They were new to each other and used to seeing new faces, it seemed. The curiosity directed at Justice seemed to be caused more by the fact that he was alone, riding an unsaddled Indian pony, than by the fact that he was a stranger. What did the Thunder Riders have to fear from a lone stranger, after all? A man who didn't belong would have to be insane to ride into their camp. They would simply overpower and kill any interloper; the idea of an enemy among them was unthinkable.

The place looked like a dirty army camp: stacked rifles; dozens of fine-looking horses; men wearing two pistols or three, decked out in crossed bandoliers. There were big ugly men and small dapper ones, all armed to the teeth, all killers willing to slaughter the innocent for a price.

"Lose your saddle?" someone called out, and Justice reined up furiously.

"Lost more than that, goddammit," he barked at the balding, hatless man in worn-down boots and leather vest over faded red shirt. The man took an involuntary step backward at Ruff's outburst, grinned toothlessly, and came ahead to stand beside the paint.

"Indian horse, ain't it?" the man asked.

"That's all I could get. Cheyenne killed my mare. Jumped me and Ellis and Sayers a few miles back. Killed them, got my horse. Got one of the bastards and now I'm riding his pony. Where's the boss?" Justice demanded.

"Hawkins?"

"Who else?" Justice said testily, and swung down from his horse to stand wiping his forehead. A few men leaning against tar-paper and plank shacks watched and listened, but no one seemed very interested.

"Thought you meant the main man," the outlaw told Justice. He was still grinning, and Justice decided he didn't have all of his nuts and bolts.

Ruff gambled, "I don't care if I ever see Todd again."

"You seen Jesse Todd personal?" the little man asked.

"Seen him, was paid by him—not that there's any of that money left."

"Women?" the little man leered.

"Some of that. What's your name?"

"Benjamin. Cy Benjamin," the little man said agreeably. "Don't I know you?"

"Don't think so. Hicks is my name."

"Kansas?"

"Colorado," Justice said, hoping that was far enough away to explain his late arrival.

"Seems like I seen you," Benjamin repeated, leaning closer so that his rank breath flooded Ruff's nostrils.

"Been to Leadville?" Justice asked. It was a town he knew well enough, should anyone start questioning him.

That didn't worry him so much; what did concern him was the chance that he would run into someone who *did* know him—like Jesse Todd.

"What's up?" Ruff turned to see a vast, black-bearded man with an expansive belly and tiny feral eyes. This one Ruff did know, not personally, but from the circulars. His name was Deke Connely, and he was bad news. He was a knife-fighter and a throat-cutter, a drinker and a thug. He had the morals of a rutting coyote and the cunning of a prairie wolf.

"Nothin'. Hicks here was telling me how his people got cut up by the Cheyenne," Benjamin said. The way he said it made it seem that he had known Hicks for some time.

"Cheyenne get you?" Deke Connely asked in a low, nearly animal voice.

"Missed me," Ruff said dryly, "got my partners."

"Too bad," Connely said in a tone that indicated he couldn't care less about any human life other than his own.

"Fist is pretty well stirred up," Justice said. "I ever get a chance to lay hands on that bastard . . ."

"Leave him for the army. Say your name is Hicks?"

"That's right."

Benjamin piped in, "Mister Todd sent for him personal."

Deke stroked his unruly, greasy beard. "That right? What're you, some kind of gunman?"

"Some say," Justice answered softly.

Deke Connely was the sort of man who was always ready to fight— and Ruff didn't want to stir him up. So far he had managed to bluff himself into a deadly, high-stakes game. He needed no one to call him.

"Hawkins around?" Ruff asked.

"Not just now." Deke Connely was still staring at Ruff, some malevolent thought working behind those tiny eyes. Then his attention was captured by someone else calling to him, and he turned away suddenly as if Ruff had never existed.

Benjamin sighed with relief. "The Deacon is enough to nervous a man," he said.

"Is he?" Ruff Justice watched Deke Connely go, then stretched, getting the kinks out. "What's around for grub?"

"Buffalo meat and beans," Benjamin said. "What else?"

"What else? Show me some," Justice demanded. Benjamin was willing to accept Hicks; he seemed the sort of man who needed a leader to follow and he was perfectly content to let Hicks assume that role.

Ruff followed him to a miserable tent that was ranker than Benjamin's breath. Foul-tasting buffalo stew and a plate of beans were ladled out willingly by the little murderer—that was what Benjamin was, or the people in charge here wouldn't have signed him on.

Who, Justice wondered, had Benjamin had the nerve to kill? Women, children? If so, those were all the credentials he needed for this bloody job. Repulsive as the little man was, Ruff would have to cultivate his friendship. It gave Hicks an aura of criminal respectability, and for a man walking on the raw edge of death, that was immeasurably necessary.

Benjamin introduced Ruff to a few of his cohorts. There was Gunnison Studdard, who talked with a lisp, shot with either hand, and had a redheaded scalp fastened to his gun belt; Big Bill Whitney, a one-eyed, lean, gray-bearded outlaw who was up from Kansas and liked to brag about the niggers he had killed when they got too uppity.

They were the dregs of the earth, not brave but bloodthirsty; not clever but cunning as animals. A gold piece would turn them on their best friend. Two would buy a woman's scalp. They were vermin and Justice wished he had a bundle of dynamite and a short fuse. A brief, fiery explosion and the earth would be cleansed a little.

Tate Hawkins rode in by midafternoon, a well-dressed

man with a pale mustache, hard green eyes, and hollow cheeks. A fire bell called the dirty little army to a meeting beside a shack encircled by mud.

"Fill your bellies and load your guns," Hawkins said. "We're riding."

Deke Connely stood beside Hawkins, savage and satisfied, ready to kill to brighten his dark existence.

"Where we riding?" Bill Whitney asked.

"Cameron Creek Station. Know it?"

Whitney shook his head. None of them were Dakota men—no Dakota man would light the brushfire these killers wanted to touch off.

"Not going through Breakheart?" Ruff Justice asked, stepping forward as eyes shifted to look at him.

Tate Hawkins' cold green eyes shuttled to Ruff's face. "Who the hell are you?" the gang leader demanded.

"Name's Hicks," Deke Connely said in a low voice, "says Jesse Todd sent for him personal."

"Is that so? Kind of late arriving, aren't you, Hicks?"

"Fist had something to say about that."

"What's it to you which way we go?"

Ruff said, "Breakheart's loaded with Cheyenne warriors—believe me, they got some friends of mine."

"They did now, did they?" Hawkins asked in a nasty tone of voice. "Mind telling me why Jesse Todd sent for you?"

"Simple," Ruff said, gambling, "I know the country and none of you boys seem to very well."

Hawkins sucked on that one for a while and Justice knew he had touched the truth. These hired outsiders didn't know Dakota Territory, and that could be his in—and maybe his only weapon against the Thunder Riders.

"Where's Todd anyway?" Justice demanded. "I understood he'd be here."

"You understood wrong, Hicks," Tate Hawkins shot

back. "I'm in charge here for now, and if you don't like it, you can ride on back to wherever the hell it is you came from!"

"I work for wages, Mister Hawkins," Ruff said with what he hoped was suitable humility. "You're boss if you say so—I was just repeatin' what I was told." He had at least learned one thing: Todd, who alone among the Thunder Riders would know who Hicks was, was not there and not expected soon.

"I want to talk to you," Hawkins said. "Later." He inclined his head toward the slanting shack beside him, and Justice nodded. "The rest of you get yourselves organized. Get your gear and plenty of bullets. Cameron Creek Station has some men."

The Thunder Riders slowly broke up, drifting toward their own tents and horses. Touched familiarly on the arm by Benjamin, Justice started toward the shack where Tate Hawkins waited for him.

Inside, it was dirty and dark, the air smelling of grease and tallow. Tate Hawkins sat in a rickety chair, filling himself with whiskey. Deke Connely was nowhere in sight, but Ruff still felt his presence. Maybe the big man was outside, waiting for a signal to kill.

"Sit down, Hicks," Tate Hawkins said, and Justice knocked a bundle of rags from another chair to sag into it, hands folded on his lap, rifle between his knees. "Where are you from anyway?"

"Leadville," Justice replied.

"Leadville. I been there, never heard of you." Tate Hawkins took another deep drink from his amber-colored bottle.

"You must not've been listening," Ruff said. He thought Hawkins was trying to bluff him and it seemed that he had guessed right. Hawkins sat there glowering at him.

He changed the subject abruptly. "Indians in Breakheart, you say?"

"Plenty of 'em. Best thing to do is swing south through Cottonwood Wash, follow the creek up to Cameron Creek Station, and do what has to be done."

"You know this country."

"That's why Mister Todd sent for me."

"Yeah." Hawkins' reply was flat, neither believing nor disbelieving. He took one last drink, corked the bottle, and tossed it aside. "I'm listening to you this time, Hicks. I'm taking your word for the way things are in Breakheart. If Fist kills half of these dumb sons of bitches, it really doesn't matter—that'll suit our purposes as well as anything else—but I'm not ready to lose 'em just yet."

Or your own life, you bastard, Justice thought. But things were beginning to go his way. The Thunder Riders had accepted him—so far—and Hawkins seemed to believe his story of having been sent north by Jesse Todd to act as a guide for the raiders.

Ruff considered briefly that he was in an ideal position to fight them—from inside their organization, where a lot of damage could be done surreptitiously. If he could avoid getting caught . . . if Jessie Todd didn't actually show up . . . if someone in this gang didn't recognize him . . . if and if.

Tate Hawkins rose. "We're riding, Hicks. You got all the gear you need?"

"I'm short. Some Cheyenne warrior is carrying most of my stuff," Ruff said.

"See Cord. He's our armorer—anyone can tell you where to find him—tell him I said to give you what you need."

Ruff got to his feet and thanked the man. There was something lingering in Hawkins' eyes, something that told Justice he still wasn't sure just *what* the man called Hicks did need.

Maybe killing.

Outside, the camp was on the move. Men with saddles slung over their shoulders stumped through the deep mud toward the strings of war horses. About half of them were wearing paint and feathers now, and Ruff's mouth tightened a little.

Benjamin caught up with him as he started across the road himself. "Where's the armorer?" Ruff Justice asked. "Man named Cord?"

"Cord?" Benjamin looked relieved and perplexed. "Over there—see that big old army tent. What happened, Hicks? I thought Hawkins was going to lay into you."

"Did, did you?" Ruff muttered as they walked together toward the armorer's tent. Justice couldn't help thinking how well-organized this outfit was. There had to be plenty of money to keep it running. He supposed there was a hell of a lot more to be made from those planned sections of land.

The tent was busy. Boxes of cartridges were slapped on the rough-sawn counter and snatched away before they settled. Men were digging into small jars of paint, having themselves a ball becoming Indians. Someone kept shouting for shotgun shells.

Ruff let himself be guided by Benjamin, who had apparently latched on to him for good, to a counter where handguns and gun belts lay for the taking.

The camp might have been slovenly, but the weapons were the best. Colt .44s and Remingtons; oiled, cut-away holsters, single or double. Ruff selected a belt and tried it on for fit, choosing a Colt that he tried for balance, slid in and out of the holster, and then loaded. Benjamin watched him quietly.

It was then that it happened. Ruff half-turned toward the center of the room and he was recognized.

The man's name was Hobie Schwartz and he was a small-time killer with big ideas. He had tried to run roughshod over certain people in Bismarck until Justice brought him up short one night in an alley. Schwartz knew him immediately. The bandit reached for his gun, dropping a blanket he had been carrying.

"Ruff," Schwartz called out, and Justice, crouching, drew and fired. Schwartz's bullet clipped wood from the counter behind Justice. Ruff's own bullet was truer.

The .44 slug burrowed into Schwartz's belly and Hobie staggered back at the impact, trying to claw the pain out. It wasn't a killing wound and Justice knew it. He shot Schwartz again, this one taking him below the collarbone on the left side, severing a major artery.

Schwartz gurgled something else and fell, twisted, to the floor. where he lay as the rest of the Thunder Riders watched. Ruff Justice walked forward, toed the body, and satisfied himself that Schwartz wasn't going to do any more talking to anyone.

Shouts and approaching footsteps turned Ruff's head. Tate Hawkins, pistol drawn, and the hulking figure of Deke Connely appeared in the tent door. They took it all in with a glance and demanded, "What the hell's going on here?"

"No man can talk to me like that," Justice answered calmly, holstering his pistol.

"Who is it?" Hawkins asked, nodding at the dead man.

"Hobie Schwartz."

"Know him, did you, Hicks?"

"Not until just now."

Benjamin was eager to put in his two cents' worth. "Schwartz drew on him, drew first, Hawkins."

Hawkins' eyes flashed briefly and then went cold. "Well, Hobie wasn't much of a loss. Why'd he do it, Hicks?"

Ruff said, "You'd have to ask him." But the dead man wasn't going to do any talking.

"Hobie wasn't much, but he was pretty fast," Hawkins mused. "Got him twice, didn't you?"

"I don't miss much," Justice said.

Hawkins studied Justice again for a long minute, then he shrugged and waved a hand. "Get him out of here. Everybody else keep moving. Watch that gun, Hicks."

"I do—as long as they leave me alone," Justice answered.

"See that you do. Deke here had the idea you were a ringer of some kind . . ." He looked at the body again. "I guess you're not."

Then the two war leaders went out of the tent, two men dragging Hobie Schwartz after them.

Benjamin was still beside Justice. Now the little man asked, "What was that he called you, Hicks?"

"It doesn't matter now," Justice said, taking cartridges, a blanket and saddle, and a little war paint from the armorer.

"Not to Hobie it don't," Benjamin said, grinning his toothless grin, "but I wanted to make sure I never said it to you."

"You heard him, didn't you?" Justice said.

"Yeah, I heard him, but I must have heard him wrong."

"Don't worry about it. Let's go—I need a horse."

"Sure." Benjamin stared at Ruff a moment longer, trying to figure it out. "Rough." That was what he had heard Hobie Schwartz say, only that, or something that sounded like that. Seemed a small reason for shooting a man. "Rough." The word settled in Benjamin's tiny brain, rattling around in the empty corridors there. Then he shrugged, picked up his own gear, and forgot about it—for the time being.

8

They rode out of the muddy camp in a long wavering line. Fifty riders moved out across the prairie, their horses' hooves drumming like thunder. Ragged, dirty, painted, they might have been a legion out of hell risen up from the netherworld to bring death and destruction.

Ruff Justice rode with them. He was just behind and beside Tate Hawkins and Deke Connely. Deke, with his huge frame and massive black beard, hadn't bothered to make himself look like an Indian. Hawkins had put on his war paint. Half of his face was crimson, the other half yellow.

This face turned occasionally toward Justice as they rode, its expression masked by paint. Justice himself had thrown a few black stripes diagonally across his face, using three fingers. Wearing buckskins, with his long hair tied back, he looked more the part than any of them, except for his drooping black mustache.

Justice guided them toward Cameron Creek Station, where Dud Tinker, his sons, wife, and daughter held down a way station and trading post behind a stockaded wall.

His idea in avoiding the shorter route through Breakheart was threefold. First, going that way would find no sign of the Indian fight Justice had supposedly been engaged in and would shatter his story. Second, by veering farther east there was a chance of meeting McCracken's posse if they hadn't given up and returned to Bismarck. McCracken wasn't smart, but he would be sure to report seeing this gang of thugs on the plains to the army. Third, approaching from the east would give Dud Tinker a better chance of spotting the incoming raiders than he would have if they burst from the mouth of Breakheart, which was directly behind his station.

Maybe none of that thinking was going to do any good. They hadn't spotted McCracken or an army patrol and they were nearly to the outpost. Ruff had done his thinking, but it didn't seem it was going to be enough to save the lives of Tinker and his family.

"How far?" Tate Hawkins demanded.

"A couple of miles."

"You know this place, Hicks?"

"I know it." Ruff had been fed and sheltered there by Dud and his friendly wife.

"How many guns?"

"Maybe a dozen. He's got three or four Arik Indians working with him, a couple of white men. It might not be all that easy—they've got a log wall around the place."

"Doesn't have to be easy," Hawkins snapped, "just has to be done."

And if a dozen people at the outpost were killed, along with a dozen of Hawkins' own men it didn't matter. The job had to be done. A war had to be started, and once it got started, the Thunder Riders could quietly sift out of the territory, their pockets lined with blood-smeared gold.

They crested the rise and sat looking through the scattered pines toward the outpost below. Smoke rose from the chimney of the main house and from the smoke shack outside the stockaded walls. Ruff could make out a hired hand, an Indian, moving around in front of the open gate.

He was performing some chore Ruff couldn't identify at that distance.

"A setup," Deke Connely said in his bear growl of a voice. "They don't have a chance. Take out that Indian—and then there's no one to close the gate."

"Studdard?" Tate Hawkins said, and the man, with his reputation as a scalp-taker, came forward. "Six men around the far side. See that gulley? At the first shots you try the back wall. Keep your paint on and make sure no one stays alive to figure out you weren't Cheyenne."

"The bodies?" the scalper asked with an unhealthy eagerness.

"Make it look good. Anyone finds them I want them to know Indians did it."

Studdard was grinning when he turned his horse, selected his men with a mute, jabbing finger, and began to circle toward the gulley behind the quiet outpost.

"Five men on that bluff," Hawkins said. "Cover us from there. Hicks, you're with them."

"I kind of wanted to go down," Justice said.

"You heard me. I'm in charge here, not you. I don't care if Jesse Todd did hire you personally."

"All right." Ruff shrugged. "Whatever you say."

Along with Benjamin and three other men Justice walked his horse to the mountain-sage-screened bluff, swung down, and took up a position with his Winchester. He placed a box of cartridges at his elbow and took a few practice sightings. One on the column of smoke rising from the house, another dead on the back of Tate Hawkins. If it would have done any good at all, Justice would have put a round through the outlaw leader's back then and there. But it wouldn't have. It wouldn't have saved a single innocent life.

Hawkins and his men were preparing themselves, stuffing their giveaway wide-brimmed hats in their saddlebags—there was always the chance that someone might do the unthinkable and survive the massacre. It had to be the Cheyenne who were blamed.

At the outpost below, the people went about their normal duties, having no idea that death hovered over them, violent, bloody death.

"What was you doing?" Benjamin asked, and Ruff realized he had held his sights on Tate Hawkins for a long while. "He rile you?"

"Just a little," Ruff answered.

"Good thing it was only me saw you," Benjamin said. He lay near to Ruff behind the sage, which was scattered across the piny hillside. "You got a quick temper, don't you?"

"Real quick," Ruff said, reinforcing the little man's opinion of him.

Benjamin was nervous. He shouldn't have been—he had been through these massacres before—but he was dry-mouthed and jittery. He was, after all, only a small man in a very big game.

Justice noticed it and decided to use it to his advantage. Looking around very casually, he let his head snap up. He touched Benjamin on the shoulder.

"What is it?" Benjamin asked. His voice was a little shaky.

"Cheyenne," Ruff said. "I thought—"

"Over there?" Benjamin laughed dryly. "It's just some of the boys moving into position."

"You're probably right." Justice continued to look in the direction in which Studdard and his men had gone. "I just thought—"

"You know Indians, don't you?" Benjamin asked. His thumb had hooked around the hammer of his Winchester, drawing it back.

"I know them. I know they were up in Breakheart yesterday. It seems . . . Never mind, probably I'm wrong."

Benjamin continued to gaze downslope. His eyes were a little too wide, his breath came a little too rapidly.

Ruff helped him along. "If the bastards ever caught us out in the open like this . . ."

"It's not Indians," Benjamin said hopefully.

"No."

"Where did you think you saw them?" the raider asked after a pause. Hawkins and the main force were ready to attack now, moving slowly forward in a picket line, ready to charge at their leader's signal. Below, the outpost continued its routine, unaware of the imminent attack.

"There!" Justice shouted, and Benjamin touched off, his rifle sending a seeking bullet into nothing, into the pines where it lost itself with a hollow ricochet. Hawkins' horse reared up, and below Ruff saw the Indian who had been working outside the station run for the gate.

Hawkins' army charged down the slope. The gate was already closing, and already rifles were firing back from the parapet Tinker had constructed around his fort. Smoke lifted silently from rifle muzzles and then the sound reached Ruff's ears. The four men around him began to fire in return.

Justice's rifle joined in.

But his sights were set on different targets. He took one Thunder Rider from his saddle, wounded another; Ruff glanced at Benjamin, but the little man, shaken now, was so busy burning ammunition that he didn't notice anything else going on around him.

Ruff sighted on Deke Connely, then lost him as the big man's horse dipped into a wash. Then he found another target and killed his third Thunder Rider of the day—without a moment's hesitation, without an ounce of regret.

From behind the outpost now Studdard and his band of men rose up to attack the back wall. Justice shot the first man forward and then shouted to Benjamin. "Looks like Studdard's in trouble. I'm going down to help him!"

Benjamin started to rise to his feet, but Justice shoved him down. "I'm going along," the small man whined.

"No. No sense in both of us getting in trouble for leaving our position."

Benjamin knew he was already in trouble, deep trouble. He had fired the first shot, alerting the outpost. Ruff's argument struck deeply, and Benjamin, with a frantic glance, settled in to snipe away at the defenders behind the outpost wall. It was an almost futile task, for only an extreme stroke of fortune was going to guide a bullet through the parapet's gaps to find flesh and blood.

Justice worked his way into the pines and began to circle. Someone shouted something, but Justice kept on going. In his Indian paint he was readily identifiable as one of the raiders' own and no one had a reason to take a shot at him.

Running flat out downslope, the rifles' echoes crashing against his eardrums, gunsmoke filling the basin, Ruff made the gulley and jogged on, weaving through the willows and sumac toward Gunnison Studdard and his force of six men—five, now that Justice had removed one vermin from their ranks.

Studdard was one man Justice wanted dead. The bastard wore that white woman's scalp as a badge of courage, and the spirit of the dead, redheaded woman cried out for vengeance.

A man with a painted face suddenly popped up before Justice. The eyes were frightened but evil. "Goddamn," the Thunder Rider said, "you scared hell out of me. Bastards almost got me once."

"Did they?" Ruff Justice said, and he shot the killer in the face, sending him sprawling back into the mass of sumac and nopal cactus behind him. Justice leapt over the body, giving the man no more thought than he would have given a dead rattler.

Ahead now, Studdard's remaining men crept toward the back wall of the outpost. Studdard himself saw Justice first and spun, gun in hand. There were too many guns for Justice to take his chance just then, so he called out instead. "It's Hicks, Studdard!"

"What're you doing here?"

Before Justice could answer, the small gate in the back fence opened and Ruff's heart leapt as he saw Dud Tinker's daughter, a brunette of seventeen or so, sprint for the gulley . . . and right into the hands of the raiders.

Studdard's eyes lighted. He reached for his knife and started after the girl. Justice was on his heels, heart racing. There was no option here. To save the girl he was going to have to kill Studdard and then he would be gunned down himself. The girl would be taken either way.

Studdard caught her at the rim of the coulee behind the stockade and leapt for her. They went down the sandy coulee slope in a tangle of limbs, petticoats, and gingham cloth. Ruff Justice was behind Studdard, sliding, slipping, tumbling down the bank in a storm of sand.

He caught up with them just as Studdard, his eyes gleaming in a painted face, lifted his scalping knife. He yanked the Tinker girl's head up by its glossy dark hair.

Justice flung himself at the badman, knocking him to the ground.

"What in hell are you doing?" Studdard screamed. His men were coming on the run, too close behind to allow Justice to finish the butcher.

When Justice spoke, his voice was matter-of-fact. "Christ, Studdard, we've got uses for a woman like this. Figure it—Indians take young women hostage. We'll keep her for a while and then finish her off."

"Horny bastard," Studdard said, but he was grinning.

"Yeah, I guess so," Ruff admitted. He helped Studdard to his feet.

The outlaw dusted himself off, and looked at the dark-haired, lovely girl sitting on the sandy ground. He winked at Justice. "You got some brains, Hicks. Stupid of me."

"Hell with that," Ruff said. "Let's finish the rest of 'em and make tracks—someone said there are Cheyenne up there."

Studdard's dark eyes flickered to the high country and his grin drooped away. "You watch her," he said. "She belongs to the two of us, I guess."

Then Studdard was gone, charging up the slope, but he left a man behind to watch. There was nothing more Justice could do just then to free the young woman, who was petrified with fear, her eyes flooded with tears. Her gaze searched Ruff's face, looking beyond the paint.

"Justice . . ." she whispered.

"Shut up. I've got to treat you hard, Donna, understand."

"They're killing—"

"Do you understand?" Ruff hissed. "They want to kill you too."

"Yes," she said, and that was the last word Ruff heard out of Donna Tinker for hours.

He let Studdard drag her back as a sort of trophy when the bandit returned, but Justice kept his eyes on her. By then the outpost was burning, smoke billowing into a cold sky. At the hill crest Tate Hawkins was fit to be tied.

"Idiots, baboons! Three of them got away. The old lady, two men. Now we'll have to track them down. Who in blazes fired that first shot?"

Hawkins, his war paint smeared and smudged, let his eyes drift across the ragged ranks of his warriors. Finally Benjamin muttered, "Guess it was me. Mister Hawkins." Benjamin looked to his friend Hicks for moral support, but Justice was standing clear of this.

"You, you stupid bastard, what were you doing?"

"Indians," Cy Benjamin said, backing up a step, blinking. He swallowed hard and waved a feeble hand. "There was Indians up there."

"Indians," Hawkins said with disgust, "the dumb shit saw Indians."

"I thought—"

"You don't know how to think. You, what are you doing with that girl?" Hawkins demanded, turning on Gunnison Studdard.

"Savin' her," Studdard said in what was nearly a childish voice. "Just figure the Cheyenne stole her off."

"Saving her? You save her for a bit, then get rid of her for good—get me?"

"Sure do, Hawkins. Sure do."

That was as far as Tate Hawkins dared to go. Ruff knew why: Gunnison Studdard had brought six men with him from Kansas. Hawkins didn't wish to cross all of them. He had proved he was boss, and that was enough. It didn't matter much if the girl was killed now or later.

What did matter was that there were three other survivors of the massacre out there somewhere. They might have been deceived by the Indian disguises—and then again, they might not have been. This was no time to take chances.

"Fan out," Hawkins said, swinging back up on his own horse, "and *find* them."

They began to look, searching the coulees and the trees beyond the outpost. Ruff rode alone, circling close to the outpost, picking up sign that the others didn't bother to look for. A small boot, a woman's boot, had left its imprint in the soft soil there.

He found another a hundred feet on and then another. Soon the tracks were lost in the coulee, but Justice had the woman's direction figured, and unless she was using a cunning unusual in these circumstances she would keep running blindly that way—south.

Ruff looked behind him, picked the pace of his horse up a little, and rode on.

It didn't take long. Half a mile on he saw gray flannel, saw a woman rise and start to run, her hands waving. Don't scream, dammit, Justice said silently.

He lifted the horse into a canter and caught up quickly, seeing a horrified pale face turn back toward him, seeing her mouth open in a silent plea.

Justice leapt from the horse's back and took the Tinker woman down in a flurry of sand, clamping his hand over her mouth. They slid to a stop, Ruff on top of the fear-crazed, struggling pioneer woman.

He held her still, keeping his hand on her mouth for a long minute as the insects in the coulee bottom buzzed around them. Seeing her eyes alter as she grew curious and a little calmer, Ruff took a chance and removed his hand. His white handprint still showed in her pink flesh.

"You're not . . . Indian," she breathed.

"No. It's Ruff Justice, Mrs. Tinker."

"Ruffin . . . Oh, God! What's happened? Why are you. . . ?"

"Did Dud get out?" Justice asked curtly.

"He's out. I don't know where. So's our son, George. My God, they've got Donna! I saw—"

"Don't worry about Donna. She'll get loose, I promise you. Mrs. Tinker, you've got to do what I tell you. The old French fort—go up there. Don't worry about Dud or your son. You get to the old fort and wait. I'll send Donna to you, with horses if I can. Then you've got to get to Fort Lincoln, you understand? Tell them that these aren't Indians at all. They're white raiders, understand me?"

"I saw . . ." The woman shook her head in confusion.

"They're white raiders and the army's got to get out here and take care of them. Tell MacEnroe he'll need at least two companies—they've got seventy riders. Do you understand?''

Ruff had to shake her a little, but the Tinker woman was made of good stuff and she had seen some hard times in her life. She finally sat up and nodded, holding her throat. ''Old French fort. Wait for Donna. Get to Lincoln. Tell the colonel he'll need at least two companies. Seventy raiders.''

''White men!''

''White men.'' She nodded.

''All right. Tell him Fist wants peace. Tell him . . . just tell him Fist wants peace and these are white raiders.'' The rest of the story could wait. For now it was imperative that the army make its way north and stop these predators.

Before many more died—too many.

''Donna. You get her free,'' Mrs. Tinker panted.

''Don't you worry about that,'' Ruff Justice said. ''I'll send her to you unharmed.''

How he would do that was another story, but Justice didn't let his worries show. He smiled, touched the woman's shoulder, and watched as she clambered up and out of the coulee, making for the ruins of the old French fort. It was north of them and he didn't figure Hawkins would be looking in that direction. Maybe he could spring Donna Tinker. And maybe the two women could get to Lincoln and bring help. Then, just maybe the river of blood could be halted.

One step at a time, Justice told himself. He glanced at the sky where day was already fading to pink and gold, then started back to rejoin the raiders and take that first step.

The last thing he counted on was meeting Cy Benjamin with a loaded, cocked rifle trained on him.

9

"You set me up," Cy Benjamin panted. He was sitting his roan horse at the top of the bluff. He was hatless, the wind lifting his thinning light-brown hair, his toothless mouth gaping open with emotion. In his hands was a Winchester, which he showed every intention of using.

Ruff walked his horse forward, his hand slowly dropping toward his holster. His voice was mild when he asked, "What's going on, Benjamin? What's the trouble?"

"Maybe I'm not smart, but I'm not stupid either," Benjamin answered. "I know what happened back there. There was no Indian around. You wanted me to fire a shot—a warning shot for the people in the outpost."

"Why would I want to do that, Benjamin?" Ruff asked.

"You tell me, Hicks—or whatever your name is."

"It's Hicks."

"Keep that hand away from your gun, Hicks—or whatever your name is. What happened back at the camp has been gnawing at me."

"Has it?" Ruff inquired smoothly.

"Yeah. You killed Hobie Schwartz. He drew first, yeah, but why did he?"

"You tell me," Justice said. His horse shifted under

him, bringing him at a slightly better angle. Benjamin was only ten feet from him, to Ruff's right side.

"I intend to. Ever hear of a man called Ruff Justice?" Benjamin's toothless grin flashed triumphantly.

Justice only shrugged. "Can't say that I have, no."

Benjamin looked briefly uncertain, but he rushed on. "I heard the name. Never seen him, but I heard the name. Supposed to be some real tough army scout up here. 'Rough.' That was what I thought Hobie Schwartz said. I didn't figure it for a name, Mister Ruff Justice."

Ruff did the last thing Benjamin expected then. He yawned. Threw up his arms and yawned, shaking his head. When he lowered his hands again, he said, "Nope . . ." and then he drew. The draw was a good one, quick and clean, the Colt seeming to leap into Ruff's hand, to stab flame and death at an off-guard Cy Benjamin, a little man without many brains who had gotten smart at the wrong moment.

Justice's .44 punched a hole through Benjamin's heart, and blood spewed from his mouth, washing down his shirtfront as he was blown back to land against the earth, his horse dancing away.

Justice looked around carefully, seeing no one. Then he holstered his Colt and shooed Benjamin's horse off toward the coulee. It would vanish there—there was even a chance Mrs. Tinker might find it and use it to get to the old fort. If she wasn't too finicky: there was a hell of a lot of blood on the saddle.

Ruff left Benjamin where he lay. Then he rode slowly back toward the main bunch of outlaws. He wondered whether there was a price on the heads of all of these bastards and how much he might have already earned.

Tate Hawkins was having a fit when Justice rode into the Thunder Riders' camp. A cold wind was guttering the small fire they had crowded around.

". . . Not a damned one of 'em," Hawkins was

shouting as Justice swung down from his horse. The outlaw leader's eyes flashed to Justice. "Hicks, you find any of 'em?"

"Not a sign," Justice said, helping himself to the coffee someone had started boiling.

"See! Damn it all, this is going to cost us another day at least. We got to find them and take care of them all." That reminded him, "Studdard, get rid of that damned girl too. Next thing you know she'll be taking off."

Donna Tinker sat on the earth, head turned, looking inert and utterly miserable. Studdard patted her on the head as if she were a found pup.

"She won't run off, Tate. Where in hell's she gonna go?"

"Where'd the others go! Dammit, do what I tell you," Tate Hawkins ordered. Then he turned, and with Deke Connely at his heels as always, he stalked to where his horse stood and began unsaddling. The day was growing short already, and instead of the relative comfort of their shack town, the Thunder Riders were going to have to spend the night on the open prairie.

Ruff eased over to where Studdard stood. The half-dozen men he had brought with him were milling around nearby, casting an occasional glance at their leader.

"Gets on his high horse, doesn't he?" Ruff Justice said, sipping his coffee.

"One day someone'll take him off it," Studdard said savagely. "The girl's gonna be fun. Where's she gonna go?"

"He's just throwing his weight around," Ruff said. "With the men he's got he knows no one's going to buck him."

"No?" Studdard's eyes sparked a little. "He can think that, but maybe he'll learn different one day."

"Maybe when that time comes," Ruff said in a lowered voice, "you'll let me know beforehand. Maybe you could use one more man. The bastard rides me too, and I don't like it."

Studdard looked at Ruff with renewed interest and answered, "Sure. I'll let you know. You're all right, Hicks." He took Donna Tinker's head by the hair and turned her face up toward him. "I might even let you have her second. Check with me after dark." And then he laughed, laughed long and hoarsely, his eyes revealing a mind that wasn't quite right. Silently Donna Tinker pleaded with Ruff Justice. He had promised, promised she would be all right, and now this maniac had her.

Ruff's eyes met hers, and his head moved in a barely perceptible nod. Then he turned away, moving through the camp toward his own horse. Dusk was settling; it was going to be an eventful night.

Justice made his bed a little away from the camp and curled up, trying to remain perfectly still. His eyes were far from still, however, and his mind was working constantly. Studdard had the girl: Studdard, who would be content to rape her and then mutilate her, maybe taking her dark scalp to decorate his gun belt.

The Thunder Riders were slowly settling. Filled with whiskey and exhaustion, they stumbled to their beds and rolled up against the chill of the plains night.

When the last man had settled, Ruff Justice rose.

He knew where Studdard was, knew that on this night he had no friends around him, wanted none. He had a woman.

Ruff circled the camp and approached it again on the folded, grassy hillock behind it. There a string of horses stood, eyes starlit, heads uplifted nervously. He cut one free and led it with him down the slope. There were guards posted, but the night was dark and they had grown casual in their duties, knowing no one would dare attack the number of guns they had.

Justice heard the muffled sounds, the gasping, the

strangled, muted cries, and he stopped, dropping the lead to the horse. He half-slid down the slope to the flat ground. His bowie knife's blade caught starlight and gleamed coldly.

Justice was a stalking cougar moving through the night shadows. He crouched, seeing his man. Studdard had a blanket over himself and his war prize. Donna Tinker was struggling fiercely, but it did her no good as Studdard yanked away the front of her blouse and buried his face between her breasts.

His head came up abruptly.

"Who in hell. . . ? Hicks! It ain't time yet. Your turn is later."

"Wrong," Ruff Justice said. "Yours is later. Much."

"Huh?" Studdard half-lifted himself, and Ruff Justice plunged ten inches of cold steel into the hot bowels of the scalper, ripping upward with the leading edge until he caught heart muscle and the bandit fell backward, Ruff's hand clamped over his mouth. Donna Tinker's mouth opened wide and Ruff thought she was going to scream. But she held it back, held it back as Ruff lay pressed against the dying Thunder Rider, feeling his death struggle, which faded away to spasmodic twitching and then ceased.

"Get the hell out of here," Ruff Justice snarled.

"I . . ." Donna Tinker was trying to cover her breasts. It was no time for modesty.

"There's a horse a hundred feet up." Justice pointed. "You can't miss it. The old French fort, you know it?" The girl nodded mutely, still clasping her breasts. "Your mother will be there. Get now. Now!" he repeated in a hiss, and the girl rose to scamper off through the night shadows.

Ruff Justice rearranged things a little. Removing his own bowie knife from the outlaw's body, he wiped it clean on the grass. His buckskins were remarkably free of blood. The little he saw he rubbed with a handful of damp grass.

Studdard's own knife was in its belt sheath still and Justice slipped it free, digging it into the wound to bloody it. The temptation was strong to try planting the knife near Tate Hawkins to see what that might stir up, but it would be too risky. The girl would have to take the blame. Ruff backed away from the corpse now wrapped in its blankets. He eased back to the ridge and worked his way back to his own bed unseen.

Dawn came early and there was an uproar in the bandit camp. Justice sat up, wondering what was going on, until he remembered, and then he just sat in his bed, smiling.

He made up his bedroll and walked to the camp, his rolled blanket shouldered, rifle in hand.

"What's up?" he asked one of the outlaws.

"Gun Studdard got himself killed. Wouldn't listen to Tate and now he's paid the price."

"Killed?" Ruff's expression was suitably shocked.

"Stupid bastard was wearing his knife. Girl slipped it from the scabbard and gutted him with it."

"Shame," Ruff said, and the man looked at him oddly. "Where's the girl?"

"Got me. Took a horse and scatted. Tate is going crazy with it all. Now he's got four people for us to find."

"We'll find 'em," Ruff said.

"Sure," the outlaw said. "Seen that!" And he pointed northward to where a new storm had begun to thunder toward them. "That means no tracks, no way to find 'em, unless they stumble into our camp."

Ruff avoided Tate Hawkins, who was now raging through the camp. He saddled up near Studdard's men, using the opportunity to add fuel to the fire.

"Who'd of thought that little girl could gut Gun like that," one of the riders said.

Ruff Justice asked, "Who says she did?"

"Huh? Goddammit, what else could've happened, Hicks?"

"I dunno." Ruff shrugged.

"What're you thinking?"

"Nothing. I don't want to make trouble."

"There's already trouble, and plenty of it." Gunnison Studdard's crew was gathering around Ruff as he tightened his cinches. "What are you thinking?"

"I didn't see Gun. Did it look like a woman did it?" Ruff asked.

"It was bad . . . There was muscle behind that. No," the man said, his eyes narrowing, "come to think of it, it didn't look like something a woman could've done. What are you suggesting?"

"Me?" Ruff swung aboard his horse. "Nothing at all. I got to work for the man."

That seed planted, Ruff turned his horse and walked it into the main camp, the outlaws following him with their eyes. Tate Hawkins was there waiting for him. The outlaw leader was in a foul mood.

"What're they saying up there, Hicks?" Hawkins wanted to know. He held the bridle to Ruff's horse and stared up at him with red eyes.

"Nothing," Ruff said vaguely.

"I want you to tell me."

Ruff looked behind him and licked his lips. Bending low, he said, "That maybe a woman didn't kill Gun Studdard. That maybe it was a man."

"What man?"

"You'd have to take that up with them," Ruff answered.

Tate Hawkins knew exactly what Ruff meant. "They think that, do they? The dumb bastards."

Justice shrugged and looked away. The storm loomed in the north. The clouds were building and had bunched together now, closing out half of the morning light. The cold, cold wind had begun again.

Tate was still glaring back toward Studdard's companions. Now a new thought penetrated his shrewd, dark mind. "Where in hell is Cy Benjamin?"

Ruff looked puzzled. He rubbed his jaw absently. "Don't know," he told Hawkins.

"Thought you were his pal."

"He thinks so," Justice said. "I don't know where he is. Last I saw him was while we were out searching for those settlers. He told me he was riding loose, said he saw Indians out there."

"The dumb little shit was seeing Indians everywhere. That's what started the mixup yesterday."

"I know it." Ruff seemed to ponder it. "Maybe, though, he was seeing Indians because they're out there."

"Cheyenne? Don't make me laugh," Hawkins said.

"Why not?" Ruff asked, pressing it. "It's their country, isn't it? Maybe they got tired of seeing us around. Maybe they've decided to get even."

A couple of men had wandered over. Big Bill Whitney, for one. Deke Connely, crouched nearby, cocked his head curiously. Tate Hawkins saw the concern on his men's faces and he tried to quell the rumor before it got started.

"The Cheyenne are runnin'. We haven't seen any for weeks."

"Benjamin said he did," Ruff insisted a little more loudly, "and where is he now? How'd those settlers get away? Maybe they didn't. Maybe the Cheyenne picked them up."

"Maybe you're getting yellow," Tate Hawkins said with irritation. He didn't need his men to start seeing Indians everywhere.

"Maybe, but I'll stick, Cheyenne or none."

"Yeah." Tate was eyeing Ruff closely now. Justice couldn't tell what he was thinking.

The first few drops of rain were beginning to fall and the outlaw's eyes lifted skyward.

Ruff's voice was casual, "When's Jesse Todd showing up?"

"You worry a lot about that, don't you?"

"He owes me money," Ruff said.

"Todd pays in advance," Hawkins said, his eyes going a little cold. Rain was spotting his brown felt hat and the shoulders of his brown coat.

"I don't figure he paid me enough," Justice said.

"Take that up with him." Looking again to the skies, Hawkins showed some anxiety. It would be tough finding those settlers now, and they had to be stopped. "Let's get up and mounted. I want you turning over rocks out there. Find those people!"

Ruff Justice said, "And keep an eye out for Indians. There just might be some around."

Hawkins gave Ruff a withering glance and walked heavily to where his own white-stockinged roan stood. Deke Connely followed after him like a massive pup—a pup with a full set of yellow fangs.

Ruff leaned back in the saddle and looked around. Big Bill Whitney was still there, peering at Justice with his one good eye. "He all right?" Ruff asked.

"Who? Hawkins? Why do you ask?" the gunman said.

"Seems like maybe he's losing it," Ruff replied. "But then, I don't know him all that well."

"Losing it?"

"He doesn't want to even think about the Indians. Everyone knows Fist is out there somewhere. The boys ought to be prepared."

"He's got other things on his mind." Whitney said.

"Like what? Gunnison Studdard?"

Whitney answered slowly, "I wouldn't know. What're you trying to do, stir up trouble?"

"Not me, Whitney. I just like to know the man I'm riding for won't knife me in my bed. I like to know the man I'm riding for has enough nerve to take on a few Indians if he has to.'' Ruff shook his head. ''I'm just not sure that Hawkins has the nerve he needs. Maybe . . . Never mind.''

''Maybe what?'' the gunman growled.

''Maybe we ought to be looking for a new leader,'' Justice said, and he started his horse away, leaving Big Bill Whitney with something to think about. When Justice next looked back, he saw that Whitney was riding among the men Gun Studdard had brought. Justice smiled and rode on.

The rain began to fall heavily and he smiled again. Whistling, he rode his horse from the camp and out onto the long plains.

10

The rain fell in heavy sheets, the wind roared across the plains. Ruff Justice stood on a low knoll staring out through the steel mesh of the rainstorm toward the flats below. Above and behind Ruff was a heavy stand of wind-battered pines. He had left his horse sheltered there when he took up his post.

He waited for a long while, eyes narrowed against the buffeting force of the storm, shoulders shaking with the cold. Then his first man came into sight and Justice settled to the ground, feeling a warmth begin to grow in his body, a glow of satisfaction.

There were two of them, Ruff saw now, moving forward on weary horses, angry and rain-soaked. Justice didn't recognize either for a minute, and he held his fire.

When he was sure of what he was seeing, he opened up with the Winchester, burning five cartridges before the men on the horses had time to blink.

The first .44-.40 slug ripped through one of the Thunder Riders' guts, tearing him open. He screamed wildly and flung out his arms. Justice's second bullet caught the other rider dead center. It was a heart shot, and he toppled from his horse to lie still against the rain-soaked earth. The other bullets were finishers, and before the echoes had died away two Thunder Riders had finished their lives of terror.

Justice crept back into the trees, unhitched his horse from the low pine bough, and rode in a long circle to the far side of the meadow. There were pines there too, and Justice moved through them as the rain slanted down.

Luck was with him. He spotted the other three riders before they saw him, and he swung down, shooing the horse away.

They were walking their horses through the pines, heads down as they searched for sign and hid their faces from the rain. Ruff went to one knee behind a moss-greened boulder and waited.

The range was thirty yards when Justice opened up, the gun jolting against his shoulder with each shot. The Winchester spoke with deadly authority. The man on Ruff's right, the one in the leather jacket, never knew what hit him as a slug ripped through his throat, dismounting him. The man in the middle drew his sidearm and fired wildly at nothing. Justice killed him coldly with two rifle bullets.

The other one started to run, and Justice lost him briefly in the trees. Cursing, Justice leapt to his feet and followed, jumping a fallen pine, dipping down into a rocky wash and out again.

The rider was beelining it toward the north. He was a hundred yards off and riding hard, bent over his horse's withers, when Justice sighted, held his breath, and fired.

The Winchester did its work. Ruff saw the horse rear up, saw the rider fall silently to the ground. The horse hobbled off but the Thunder Rider would never rise again.

Turning, Justice started back upslope. The two dead men there lay close together, rain waxing their faces, their eyes open. Justice leaned his rifle up against a tree and unsheathed his bowie. The carving up didn't take long. When it was done, Justice had two scalps he didn't know what to do with. He wiped off the knife on the pine needles and sheathed it again. Making his way farther upslope, he retrieved his horse, which shied at the scent of blood, at the sight of the human scalps.

Ruff swung aboard and rode out of the trees. He espied a hollow oak, frowned, and held the horse up, tucking the scalps inside. They would make good nesting material for a squirrel. Who said the Thunder Riders had never contributed a thing to the world?

Ruff rode northward himself, moving slowly through the rain, which now fell so heavily that he could barely make out anything past his horse's ears.

Big Bill Whitney appeared suddenly in front of Justice, rifle ready, cocked. He recognized Ruff then and lowered his weapon.

"Damn, Hicks, you scared hell out of me."

"Want something to scare you," Ruff said, "I got jumped by some of Fist's renegades back there. They damn near got me."

"Damn near—count yourself lucky. They found Walker and Graves over west of us. Both killed."

"Benjamin wasn't so crazy after all," Ruff said, looking around them through the driving rain. "He said there were Cheyenne out there."

"Yeah, and we can't even see 'em in this," Whitney complained.

"Why not ride back to the shack town, sit this out? Those settlers aren't going anywhere with Fist's people out here."

"I'd like to," Whitney said, blowing on his hand to warm it. "At least I've got a bed and a bottle back there."

"This is hopeless," Justice said. "All that's going to happen is we'll all get ourselves killed."

"Tell Hawkins that."

"Not me," Justice said. "I don't want to end up like Gunnison Studdard."

Whitney was silent. His horse tossed its head and he settled it, his single eye peering at the rain, at Justice. "Think he really did it, do you?" Whitney asked. "Think Hawkins killed him?"

"I think," Ruff Justice said with a thin smile, "that I'd better not say any more about it."

Whitney nodded. Decisively he said, "Hell with this—it's useless. Let's start north."

"Toward the camp?"

"Toward the shack town. We see Studdard's boys we'll ask 'em along. If Hawkins don't like that, he can try killing us all—or sicking that tame bear of his on us."

"Deke Connely."

"That's who I mean. How'd you like to be the mother that bore that thing?"

Ruff laughed out loud. More soberly he said, "I wouldn't want to tangle with him, I know that. He'd tear a man's head off for Hawkins."

Whitney patted his rifle. "There's not a man living that this can't put down for keeps."

"You might have to do it if you want to take Hawkins' place," Justice said. Whitney was already beginning to perceive himself as a leader; Justice was just giving him a little push now and then.

"If I have to," Whitney said grimly, "I will. He won't be the first man I've planted."

Ruff lifted a pointing finger. Three men were approaching them from the northeast. Studdard's men. They turned toward Justice and Whitney.

"What's up?" one of them wanted to know.

"We're riding back to the shack town. Coming along?" Bill Whitney asked.

"Hawkins say to?"

"Maybe Hawkins isn't going to tell us what to do anymore," Whitney answered. He touched his eye patch, adjusting it. The Studdard men were silent for a time, exchanging glances.

"You going along, Hicks?"

"I figure I'd better," Ruff said. "Hawkins has got a mad on at me . . . I don't want to sleep out."

That one touched home with the Studdard riders. "Cold out here anyway," one of them muttered.

"We'll go with you—this is foolishness."

"All right." Whitney sat a little straighter in his saddle. "Let's get on north, then."

"Mind waiting for Cowsill and Kent? They were going to meet us by the big rocks."

"We'll wait," Whitney said. He looked at Ruff Justice; it was a brief look, but a bold and triumphant one. The new leader was slowly gathering his army.

Cowsill rode in an hour later. With him was Kent, a crooked little man with a bent nose. They were cold and pale. "Jesus," Kent said, swinging down. "Indians everywhere. They got Tobin and Bud Smith. Scalped 'em."

Ruff shook his head unhappily. "I saw half a dozen up on the ridge," he said. "They damn near got my hair."

"Hawkins don't know what he's doing," Cowsill said. He was big, blond, and sour.

"That's what we figure. We're riding back to the shack town with Whitney."

Cowsill's malevolent little eyes flashed to Whitney and then flickered away. "All right," he said. "After what the bastard did to Gun, I can't ride for him no more anyway."

"It'll mean trouble," Whitney told them.

"What's trouble?" Kent asked, and the Thunder Riders laughed. Trouble was where they lived. They walked past the gates of hell six times a day.

One of these times a horny hand was going to stretch

out and drag them in. But not today—for today they were immortal, today trouble was a game.

"Let Hawkins go hang," Cowsill muttered. "If he thinks I'm riding these hills anymore today—and I mean the hell with the Indians, I'm freezin' my butt off."

"Try this." Kent had produced a bottle of whiskey from his saddlebags and Cowsill took it, laughing.

"Why you hold-out runt!" he said, and he poured a healthy swallow down his throat.

"That won't go far," Whitney said. "But I know where to get plenty more. Let's ride out of here."

They moved northward in a tight, rain-soaked bunch, the wind blowing in their faces. Ruff Justice spent his time buried in his own thoughts. He had done some good that morning, but it wasn't enough, couldn't be enough. He had killed a half a dozen of these butchers, but they had over sixty men left. He had caused a rift in the outlaw band, but that might or might not bear fruit—whoever ran the outfit, the Thunder Riders would continue to kill.

He could only hope to hang on until the Tinker family reached Fort Lincoln—if they made it there at all. Hold on and hope the army didn't take to the field and attack Fist. If that happened, the blood that the Thunder Riders had spilled would be nothing, a drop in a bucket of crimson gore.

There had to be a way to do something more . . . but what? Justice was fighting with all he had, but he just didn't have the resources. A man here, a man there, and still there were more riders. More killers on the plains, their horses' hooves drumming the earth like thunder as the lightning of their guns cut down the innocent.

It wasn't a very cheery line of thought and Justice did his best to block it all out as they rode on through the rain and the low, obscuring clouds, northward to the shack town.

There were only a handful of men there, some laborers

and the man who ran the gunmen's armory. Most of the men were hidden away in their windblown, patched tents or in their battered shacks.

The outlaws were happy and pleased with themselves. They had shelter now and whiskey. It took more than that to make Ruff Justice happy.

"Come on, Hicks, let's have a drink," Whitney called as they dismounted in the rain, the mud deep underfoot.

"I'm going to catch some sleep," Justice answered.

"Whatever you want. Hawkins'll be crazy by now. He won't know if we ran off or the Indians ate us." That pleased Whitney and he laughed at his own remark, tramping through the mud, an arm over Cowsill's shoulder. They went into the store, where the armorer lifted puzzled eyes to the Thunder Riders. Then the wind banged the door shut and Ruff was cut off from the scene.

He turned away thoughtfully, took his horse's reins, and led it to the stable, the only building that had been constructed with any care at all. He rubbed the horse down, grained it, and stood in the open doorway, hands on his hips, watching the heavy rain fall.

It was a while before his eyes fell on the can of strychnine beside the stable door. They must have had trouble with rats here—perhaps prairie dogs digging holes to menace a horse's legs.

Ruff looked a long while at the big green can with the red skull and crossbones. Then, crouching, he shouldered it and went to the back door of the stable.

It was brutal, but he was running out of ways to fight these bloody killers. Ruff started through the rain toward the water barrels behind the store. Inside, Whitney and his new recruits were laughing it up. The whiskey was flowing.

"Amount of water they drink maybe this won't work at all," Justice muttered. Nevertheless he pried the wooden covers from all six water barrels with one hand and from the can on his shoulder poured a generous dose of poison into each one. He replaced the lids and went back through the rain to the stable. Putting the can back on the floor, Justice crossed the street and went into one of the drier tents. There he lay on a cot, tugged the blanket up under his chin, and arms folded, went to sleep with the rain driving down.

It was dark when he awoke again. He sat up, rubbing his head, and stared at the damp earth floor of the tent. Something had awakened him . . . his head had come sharply up. Riders must be coming into camp. That would be Hawkins, and he would be in a blistering rage.

He was. Justice could hear the outlaw leader's voice cutting through the wind like a fiery knife even before he emerged from the tent. And just what was going to happen to all of them now? Tried as deserters? Not likely. Hawkins wouldn't want to lose seven men even if he felt like shooting them all. All they had done was come in out of the rain—something the rest of the Thunder Riders no doubt wished they had done hours ago.

Was Big Bill Whitney ready to play his hand yet? Maybe. Justice stepped outside to see the fireworks.

It was clearing, the night very cold, with a silver moon peering through the clouds. Justice stepped outside and a pair of massive arms suddenly wrapped around him.

Justice banged his skull back, trying to break the nose of whoever held him, but that only produced a dull grunt. "Easy, Hicks, or whatever your name is," Deke Connely said, and Justice knew there was no point in struggling.

A moment later Tate Hawkins appeared in front of Ruff, handgun drawn and cocked.

He jabbed the muzzle of his pistol into Ruff's belly savagely and lifted first Justice's Colt and then his bowie, looking closely at the knife.

"What are you going to do, arrest us all?" Justice asked.

"Just you."

"What makes me special?" Ruff asked. He looked to his left then and he knew.

"Hello, Justice. Caught up with you at last," Jesse Todd said. He was wearing a rain slicker and a cover over his hat, and was lighting a cigar as he spoke. "I guess they'll give me a pat on the back for taking you in."

"Alive?" Ruff asked with a crooked smile.

Todd just shook his head. "I don't think so."

Deke Connely still had his bear's arms wrapped around Justice so tightly that it was cutting off Ruff's breathing. He asked casually, "Want me to keep squeezing, Mister Todd? It'll save a bullet."

"No. I want to keep him till morning. The boss shows up then. She'll want to talk to him."

She? Ruff knew then that his guesses had been right. The boss was coming. She had to be the senator's daughter. So the dead girl had been Becky Tandy, and Ada Sinclair, for whatever reason, was behind the Thunder Riders. And her father? Justice might never find out now. Maybe Ada wouldn't feel much like talking to him when she arrived. She had already shown herself to be quick on the shoot.

"You talked to the Indians, didn't you?" Jesse Todd demanded, stepping nearer. Ruff didn't answer immediately and the easterner backhanded him viciously. "I asked you a question."

"Yeah, I talked to Fist," Ruff said. "He'll be in about midnight."

"Cocky bastard," Todd said, and he hit Ruff again, this time with a full fist, flush on the jaw. Ruff let himself sag. "Is he out?" he heard Todd ask.

"Think so, Mister Todd," Deke Connely replied. He shook Ruff a little. "Want to keep him alive?"

"Just for tonight. Got a place that'll hold him?"

"We've got a place," Hawkins said, and he said it with deep satisfaction.

"All right, then—lock him up and let's go talk to these other renegades of yours. I'll make it plain that if they want any more pay they're working for you, Hawkins."

Ruff, still playing possum, was shouldered by Deke Connely, who carried him off as easily as if he were a child. They stopped and Justice heard a lock being opened. He opened one eye, but before he could make anything out in the darkness, Deke threw him inside and locked the door.

The fall jolted Ruff and he rose, shaking his head. He was in a pitch-black storage shed of some kind. He put a hand to the walls and found them solid. Outside, a guard would be taking up his position.

It looked as though Justice had used up his cards. He sagged against the wall and sat on the cold, hard floor to wait for morning. To wait for the blonde who wanted to kill him.

11

The night dragged past. Sometime later it rained again for a while—a brief, lashing storm that hammered against the storage shed where Ruff Justice waited for his judge and jury. Distantly he heard a human cry. Someone in terrible pain. Then that sound fell away and there was nothing but the constant howling of the prairie wolves.

Several times during the night Ruff tried to find a weakness in the shed, but discovered none. Once he tried luring his guard to the door with curious tappings and groans. No one took the bait.

Hours later, Ruff heard the horses making their way into the camp. Three or four of them, he guessed. He went to the door and listened. Muffled voices came to him through the heavy planks.

". . . Supposed to find this damned place?"

"It hasn't moved any." That was Jesse Todd.

"Haven't you got someplace warm?"

And *that* was a woman's voice. Ruff didn't have to see her to know who it was. Ada Sinclair had come to inspect her troops. And to preside over an execution.

Todd said something else that Justice didn't get above the howl of the wind, and then Ada Sinclair spoke again, with obvious pleasure.

"Here? You . . . the buckskinned bastard."

"After a while we can—"

"After a while, hell," Ada Sinclair snapped. Her voice and manners had altered quite a bit since Justice had squired her around Bismarck.

Ruff stood back from the door, waiting. He considered making a fight of it, but bare hands against six-guns and Winchesters didn't seem to make much sense. He had done all he could: he had tried to break the Thunder Riders, and had gotten the Tinker family on the trail to Lincoln. Punching someone now wasn't going to gain anyone anything.

The door burst open and they tramped in, carrying lanterns. Behind them the wind gusted, working against the tents. Jesse Todd led the way inside triumphantly, his lantern held high, illuminating his sharp features.

Behind him stood the smug and beautiful Ada Sinclair, wearing a riding cape of dark green and a green hat. The rain had taken some of the curl out of her blond ringlets, but otherwise she might have been entering some grand ballroom, turning heads as she walked down some marble staircase.

"Bastard," she said, destroying that image entirely. She stepped forward and slapped Ruff across the face, a hard, stinging blow that hurt her hand with its violence.

"Good evening, Miss Sinclair," Justice said, and he bowed from the neck.

Ada looked as if she'd like to try hitting him again—with something harder—but instead she lowered her hand. A faint smile formed on her full, curved lips.

"You're going to die, Justice," she said.

"Most of us do, sometime."

"Tonight. And painfully."

"Always the perfect hostess," Ruff Justice said. If the woman was trying to scare him, she had come to the wrong man. Ruff knew fear, knew it intimately; he had walked a hard country for a long while, always knowing that death was beyond the next ridge somewhere, down in the coulee. He didn't have to face death with the surprise some men do, with the disbelief, the sense of shock that it can actually happen to them. Ruff knew it could happen at any time. Well, apparently the time had come.

"A brave, brave man," Ada Sinclair said cynically.

Ruff didn't respond.

She stood there a moment longer, glowering at him, then she turned to Jesse Todd. "Isn't there someplace else to talk? I don't want to stand around this shed."

Tate Hawkins asked, "Why talk to him?"

Deke Connely was at his shoulder, his bear's head wagging from side to side as if waiting to be unleashed by its master.

"There's the store," Todd suggested. "We can find something to drink and you can have your chat. Tie him up," Todd snapped, and Tate Hawkins moved behind Ruff to do it himself, strapping his wrists together so tightly that the rawhide strips nearly disappeared in Ruff's flesh.

"Got that tight enough?" Ruff grunted, and Hawkins kicked him behind the knee. Ruff went to the floor of the shack and stayed there until the huge hands of Deke Connely yanked him up again.

Ruff was swung around and pushed out the open door of the shack. The wind was biting. Scattered rain fell from the high broken clouds. Again a cry of pain sounded from somewhere across the camp, a gasping, frantic moan.

"What in hell is that?" Jesse Todd demanded.

"Big Bill Whitney. Says his gut is burning up," a man said.

"Too much bad whiskey," Hawkins said.

Or, Ruff considered, too much bad water. That thought gave him a little satisfaction as they half-dragged, half-pushed him along through the mud toward the store. A few Thunder Riders were still there, still drinking.

"Scatter," Hawkins said, and with some grumbling the riders did.

The door was opened and the small party entered. Tate Hawkins removed his rain slicker and sagged into a chair. Deke Connely shoved Justice to the floor and stood aside. Jesse Todd held a chair out for Ada Sinclair—nothing like a gentleman.

Ruff had a hard time rising without the use of his hands, but he made it to his feet, found a chair, and sat down, his long dark hair in his eyes.

"You saw Fist," Ada Sinclair said. It was an accusation.

"That's right," Ruff admitted.

"Now he's killing our men—" She looked sharply at Jesse Todd. "That could work to our benefit as well. Have someone take some of those bodies into Bismarck."

"You are a coldhearted bitch, aren't you?" Justice said.

Todd rose to hit him but Ada held him back, laughing.

"Yes, I guess I am."

"Does your daddy know what you do in your spare time?" Ruff asked.

"The good senator," Ada said with unconcealed venom. "No, he doesn't know. He'll continue to muddle along trying to find a solution to the Indian problem when we already have a good one."

"Kill them all."

"That's right." Ada Sinclair glanced around the store. "I thought you said we had something to drink here, Jesse."

"Whiskey. A bottle or two of wine from the wagon train."

"I'll try that."

Justice had hoped she would ask for water. It would have been a pleasure to watch this little viper poison herself in front of him.

Todd signaled to Hawkins, who rose stiffly and went looking for the wine.

"What did Fist say?" Ada Sinclair demanded.

"That he wants peace," Ruff answered.

"Peace!" She spat the word out. "They don't know what peace is. All they know how to do is kill and keep killing. Fine, let them take it in return. Every single man, woman, and child."

"So that a pack of land developers can move in?" Ruff asked.

"So that decent hardworking people can move in."

"Oh, so you're just a benefactor of the landless, trying to help the needy."

"I am here," she hissed, "to kill Indians."

There was something not quite right about those green eyes. Ruff wondered why he hadn't seen it before. The lady was plain mad.

"They came," Ada Sinclair said as if to herself. Todd poured her a glass of wine and she paused, taking a drink. "They came. I was very small, but I remember. They came and they killed my family. Killed my mother and my baby sister. Killed them!

"Then Dad hated Indians and he went hunting them. Cotton Sinclair, the Indian fighter!" She burst out in wild laughter. "So famous that they elected him to the Senate . . . and then he seemed to forget about all that."

Her eyes were wandering. She turned the glass of wine, studying it. Someone cried out with pain again and Todd looked toward the door with annoyance.

"He forgot?" Ruff prodded.

"He forgot. My father forgot. My father's hair turned white and his eyes began to close. He started talking about a 'fair settlement' so that these massacres wouldn't happen. He had just . . . forgotten. My mother," she said under her breath so that Ruff had to read her lips.

"You never forgot," Ruff said.

"I never forgot," she shouted, and her fist banged the table. "Never forgot, never forgot! When Father decided to come west to look into things, I saw my chance. All I needed was some money and Jesse Todd's friends had plenty. They wanted the land without Indians on it—I just want a world without Indians in it. It's worked out," she said with a purr, "quite well."

"Except that a lot of innocent people have been killed. You've turned these jackals loose on the people of Dakota, massacring whites yourself, doing what was done to you, leaving the territory open for a new and damned bloody war."

Ada only shrugged. The lady sipped her wine and shrugged. "I didn't do a very good job with you, did I? Who was the Indian woman?"

"One of Fist's people."

"They said Fist would talk to you, only to you. I decided to make sure he didn't. I hadn't quite decided what to do with you: take you on a picnic and have you butchered by Cheyenne Indians maybe, or simply say you had attacked me in that hotel room."

"You think nice thoughts, lady," Ruff muttered.

"It wasn't anything personal, Mister Justice," she said, and looked surprised that Justice could take it that way. "It just had to be done."

"Oh," Ruff said with irony, "I understand. If you had to kill me and half the whites in Dakota, it was all worthwhile if you could eventually kill all the Indians as well."

"That's right," she said amiably.

"You killed that saloon girl as well."

"I had help." She looked at Todd. "That *was* a clever idea, wasn't it? Jesse just happened to see her one night. All that worked out rather well."

"Why keep talking to this scout?" Jesse Todd asked.

"It's not entertaining and he hasn't got anything else to tell us. Let's get rid of him—and do it right this time."

"Yes," Ada Sinclair said, finishing her wine. "You're quite right, Jesse. It's late and I'm tired."

"Going to kill me before you turn in?" Ruff asked the lovely, green-eyed, voluptuous, so-hard woman.

"I don't think I'll try it again. Let someone better at it do it. Painfully, I think."

"Let me have him," Deke Connely said in his bearlike voice, and Ada Sinclair looked at the huge Thunder Rider as if she had never seen him before. "I'll make sure it's slow. I'll make sure he's good and dead."

"Oh." She waved a hand. "Do whatever you like." She was bored with the conversation, with trying to make the decision. "If Jesse wants you to have him, take him. As for me,"—she yawned daintily, patting her mouth with her small, pale hand—"I'm going to get some sleep. It's been a long ride and we've got to start thinking about Wickenburg in the morning. If that doesn't ignite the army, nothing will."

She rose then, lifted her skirts a little to clear the floor, smiled at Ruff Justice as if it had been a lovely party, and walked out of the store. Jesse Todd followed right behind, with a lantern.

Before Todd closed the door again, he nodded to Hawkins. The decision had been made. Get on with the execution.

"Take him," Hawkins said to his giant cohort. "And do it right."

"You ever see me fail?" Deke Connely said.

Hawkins poured himself a glass of whiskey and leaned back in his chair to sip and doze.

"Take a chaser with that," Ruff said, "it's better for your health."

Hawkins gave him a blank look. Deke Connely stalked across the room and lifted Justice from his chair. Holding him by his bound wrists, he guided Ruff to the door, opened it, and shoved him out into the cold and drizzling night. A few stars winked in the gaps between the clouds and Justice stood watching them.

"Come on," Deke said, pushing Ruff again.

"Now you get to have your fun," Ruff said.

"That's right," Deke said with pleasure. He was, after all, only a bear-voiced little boy who liked pulling the wings off butterflies and wrenching the arms off men.

A cry of pain rang out again and then another from a different tent. "I'm dying!" a man moaned.

"Bad whiskey," Ruff said.

"I never drink it," Deke Connely confided. "Just good cool water. Keeps me strong."

"Glad to hear it," Justice said. "Drink plenty."

"Huh?" Deke's slow brain turned that around for a moment and found no meaning in it. He shoved Justice onward.

"Where we going?" Justice asked as they walked from the camp into the dark of the night.

"Somewhere where it won't bother anyone," Deke Connely answered. "Hate to wake everybody up."

"Nice of you. You're a hell of a nice guy, Deke."

Deke's fist came around suddenly, savagely from behind. It landed solidly beside Ruff's jaw and Justice went sprawling, nearly blacking out as the pinwheels in his head lit up like the Fourth of July.

No one had said Deke Connely couldn't hit.

They were among the oaks now, a hundred feet from the nearest shack, and Deke decided that was far enough. He jerked Ruff to his feet.

"Untie my hands, Deke," Ruff panted. "Let's see what you can really do."

"No. I'd like to, Justice, I truly would. I'd like to take you on and pound you to powder, but I'm taking no chances. They say you're pretty slippery."

"Yellow?" Ruff asked, and the big man hit him again. Ruff managed to turn his head as the hook came in, but it still landed with enough force to shake Justice to his toes. "Is that all you got, Deke?" Ruff asked, spitting out a mouthful of blood. He wanted to rile the big man, goad him into making a mistake, but Deke was having none of it.

Now a long, narrow-bladed knife was in his hand. "You ready, Justice? Just make believe I'm a Cheyenne. Just make believe I want that long hair of yours for my squaw."

Justice was woozy. The stars in the trees swam past. The wind was cold, the oaks rustled with its gusting force. This was it. He just wasn't going to win this time.

That didn't mean he was going out without a try.

Deke Connely came forward, his hulking shoulders bowed. Ruff kicked out at his groin, but Deke slapped the foot away as if Justice were a child. He was smiling now, damn the big bastard.

"I'm going to cut you into chunks that'd be right for a stewpot, Justice. Scatter you all over hell for the coyotes."

He stepped in, knife slashing upward. Justice jerked away, feeling the knife rip through the sleeve of his buckskin shirt, tearing flesh. Hot blood flowed down his arm. Deke was on top of him now and Justice did the only thing he could do: he butted the big man in the face, cracking his skull against nose and mouth. Deke Connely staggered back a step, wavered, and then fell flat on his face in the mud.

There was an arrow sticking out of his back, and Ruff crouched, looking around. It was another minute before Spring Walker emerged from the shadows beneath the trees.

"Only this one?" she asked.

"Yes," Ruff panted. His arm was afire with pain.

"Then you should have killed him. Why wait for a woman to do it?"

"I was just playing with him," Ruff said through the pain. "Another minute . . . I would have killed him easy."

"Yes, I thought so. I ruined the game," she said, and Ruff couldn't decide whether she was serious or not.

"Cut me loose, Spring Walker. There's his knife."

"Then we will kill many more?" she asked, picking up the narrow knife and stepping behind Ruff.

"Then," Ruff Justice said, disappointing the woman, "we will run like hell."

"You?" Spring Walker frowned. Justice didn't sound much like a man of legend just then.

Ruff pulled his arms free of the thongs and rubbed his wrists. Blood flowed down his sleeve and into the palm of his hand.

"He cut you?" Spring Walker asked.

"Only once. You could have killed him a little sooner, you know."

"Is it bad?" Her voice was quieter, more concerned.

"We'll look later. For now let's get out of here—fast."

"You are running, I don't like that." She shook her head with great sadness.

"Yes, I'm running. There's a place we have to run to, Spring Walker. Not far east there's a white settlement called Wickenburg. It's there now . . . it might not be tomorrow. The Thunder Riders are going to attack it. Now, then, get your horse and let's ride."

Ruff watched her scurry off into the trees and he stood there, lips drawn back as he clutched his arm tightly, trying to stem the flow of blood. It was bad, worse than he had thought. His head swam and his knees were beginning to shake. It was not at all certain that he was going to make Wickenburg in time to prevent a massacre; there was no guarantee that he was going to live through the night. And Spring Walker, damn her, was taking far too long. He watched the trees where she had disappeared, and finally started that way. Then he heard the woman's scream and he tried to move more quickly, his arm alive with pain, his legs wobbling, the slender knife in his hand all he had to deal with the Thunder Riders.

Spring Walker screamed again and the shouting began in the camp. Ruff Justice ran on—and then he fell. Fell to lie against the cold, rain-soaked earth, the life bleeding out of him.

12

Justice got once to his feet and fell again. He moved on desperately, half-dragging himself, stumbling and slipping toward the sound of the woman's voice.

It was Bert Cowsill who had her, Bert Cowsill who lifted her, grinning, and spun her off the ground. He didn't see the buckskin-clad demon rising from the ground, knife slashing out until it was too late.

The knife took Cowsill in the right kidney and the badman fell back, a scream howling from his mouth as he clutched at his back with both hands, losing his grip on Spring Walker.

Now other men were coming on the run, bursting out of their tents in all stages of dress, some in long johns, boots, and hats.

Cowsill was wearing a Colt revolver and Justice yanked it from the still-writhing, still-screaming man's holster. He put four rounds into the knot of pursuing Thunder Riders, heard a roar of pain, and saw them rapidly retreat. Breathing raggedly, Ruff ripped off Cowsill's gun belt and pushed Spring Walker ahead of him.

"Run!"

"He caught me . . ."

"Run, I said. Move or we'll die here." Justice shoved her again, following her through the oaks to where her paint pony stood. Spring Walker bounded onto its back, going over its haunches. Ruff mounted more slowly, painfully. Spring Walker heeled the paint sharply and it leapt into motion, reaching a dead run in three strides. A shot rang out from somewhere behind them, but it wasn't close at all.

Ruff clung to Spring Walker's waist, buckling the gun belt on with one hand. The jolting of the horse racked his body with pain. He grunted once and she turned her head.

"Your wound. You are all right?"

"Don't slow up. We need some distance between us."

They needed some distance, all right, and a lot of it. Ruff had hoped to get out of that camp unseen, unheard, but it hadn't worked out that way. Now the Thunder Riders knew what had happened, and Hawkins and Todd would be lashing them into motion.

Ruff was riding double with the Cheyenne girl and he was hurt. How far could they go before the Thunder Riders tracked them down? The answer seemed to be not far enough. To the west was a confused maze of broken, pine-stippled hills. There, perhaps, they could lose their pursuit. But Wickenburg lay to the east, across the flat, featureless plains. And sleeping on this night, Wickenburg had no warning that the Thunder Riders were going to sweep down upon the town and burn it to the ground.

"That way," Justice said, touching Spring Walker's shoulder.

They had come to a river ford and the woman had slowed her pony to walk it across. She looked to the hills beyond the river, to the tangled, twisted jumble of them and then to the east.

"Yes," she said quietly, and she started the paint pony that way through the endless, stormy night.

The hills gave way to hillocks and then to rolling, endless prairie. The clouds seemed to have given up their great battle and had begun to drift southward. The moon rose late, silvering the long grass. The pony plodded wearily on.

Ruff Justice was sitting the pony's back, leaning heavily against Spring Walker, and then he wasn't. He opened his eyes to find the horse standing beside him, Spring Walker crouched over him. The sleeve of his buckskin shirt had been cut away and now it was wrapped in a cloth Ruff didn't recognize until he saw that Spring Walker had taken the sleeve off her own blouse and made a crude bandage from it.

He sat up, his head reeling, gut knotting with nausea. "All right," he said, "let's go."

"No. You can go nowhere," Spring Walker said.

"The hell I can't." Justice tried to rise, made it as far as his hands and knees, and had to stop there, his body trembling from exhaustion and lack of blood.

"You see?" Spring Walker chirped. She was crouched, her hands folded together on her lap. "You can go nowhere. I will find a shelter."

"You will," Ruff Justice said through gritted teeth, "help me get to my feet, lady. Don't argue about it, do it."

"No."

"Then go on alone, damn you. Ride to Wickenburg, and if they don't kill you on sight, tell them the Thunder Riders are coming."

She hesitated, sighed, and said, "I will not leave you," and she helped Justice struggle to his feet. He had to lean against the horse to keep from falling, but finally he was on board again, behind Spring Walker, who guided the weary little pony eastward.

Somewhere in front of them was Wickenburg. And somewhere behind, closing in very fast, were the Thunder Riders.

"You are not smart or brave," Spring Walker said as if speaking to herself and not to the man who rode behind her, arms wrapped around her waist, head against her back, "but only stubborn. Stubborn and too crazy to know when they have beaten you."

Ruff grinned through the pain. The lady had him pegged, all right. "I been trying to tell people that for years," Justice said. Stretching out, he managed to kiss the nape of her neck once, gently.

Spring Walker shook her head. "Just stupid stubborn." And those were the last words she said for hours.

Justice rode with her, half-dozing, awakened at times by jagged, searing pain.

Suddenly it was very bright—too bright—and when Justice looked up, he saw the sun beginning to rise, saw the long orange arms of dawn stretching out to gather the dark plains to it. The pony was staggering with exhaustion. There was no sign of Wickenburg anywhere.

"I will walk," Spring Walker said suddenly, and she got to the ground, leading the pony on. It wasn't enough. The horse could go no farther, although Spring Walker cussed it and beat it and pleaded with it. There was nothing to do but leave it standing there, his head hanging, and stagger on afoot.

The sun was hot on their faces, blinding them. They clambered down the sandy slope of a deep coulee and Justice barely made it up the far side. He walked on in a dream, his head humming, arm throbbing. Once he stumbled and Spring Walker had to hold him up until he could get his balance again.

"Stop," she told him, "rest." But he shook his head and continued on toward Wickenburg. "Oh, no!" Spring Walker's words were anguished. Ruff turned his head, and looking over his shoulder he saw them too.

A long line of riders, horses and men black against the distances. They were coming. The Thunder Riders had spotted them, and there wasn't a damn place to hide, no way in hell to fight them off.

"What do we do now?" Spring Walker asked. They stood close together, facing the approaching riders. The wind shifted her dark hair. Ruff kissed her on the lips and told her.

"Get out of here. Now. You're fleet afoot. Get into the coulee and run."

"And leave you?"

"And leave me. I'm not going to outrun anyone. I'll cover you the best way I can for as long as I can. I'll take a couple of them with me anyway."

"Man of legend . . ." Spring Walker started to object. Her eyes searched his ice-blue eyes, studied his face. The Thunder Riders were near. The earth shook with the sounds of their horses' hooves and the drumming sound was like rising thunder.

"Get out of here," Justice said harshly. "They're going to kill me, Spring Walker. At least let me have the satisfaction of knowing that my death will mean something, that I gave you your life."

"Man . . . I am glad we slept together," she said. Then she kissed Ruff and started away at a run, her skirt held high, dashing toward the coulee with the quick, bounding stride of a young deer.

Ruff settled to the earth, placed his gun belt with its spare cartridges behind him, checked the Colt again, and waited.

He could no longer see Spring Walker, and with luck they hadn't seen which way she had gone. The Thunder Riders, Ruff now saw, were riding double and even triple. Some of them had at least been conscientious enough to water their horses before they started. That strychnine-laced water Ruff had left as a parting gift.

"Too bad," he muttered, "that it had to be wasted on horses."

The riders slowed as they reached the coulee. Three or four rifles spoke at once as they spotted Justice flat on his belly, waiting for them, but it was a lousy angle for hitting a man and they gave it up. Ruff recognized Tate Hawkins now, and Todd, but the woman wasn't there.

The range was still too long for his handgun and he waited as the riders began to work their horses down the coulee bluff, sending up spurs of sand. As they emerged from the coulee, Ruff two-handed the Colt and waited, the hammer drawn back.

The first man up out of the coulee took a .44 slug from the blue barrel of Justice's Colt in the guts, and he and his horse both fell back into the coulee. The horse reared up, whickering loudly and crashing into another rider on his way up the bank.

Ruff shifted his sights, missed as a rider ducked low. He cursed and fired again, hitting an arm. The bullet had caught bone and shattered it. The rider yelled in pain, clutched at his already blood-soaked sleeve, and turned his horse away—directly into the path of an oncoming rider. Both men, both horses, went down. One of the horses rose again, one of the Thunder Riders. He made a mad dash back for the safety of the coulee and Justice let him go.

He had another target in his sights.

Todd had appeared to Ruff's right and the Easterner, like a general with no idea of joining the charge himself, urged his men on by waving his rifle in the air and shouting from the back of his white-stockinged sorrel.

Ruff shot Todd, the bullet seeming to nick his throat or perhaps the shoulder near the collarbone. That was enough for Todd anyway; the general took to his heels, leaving his men to charge ahead.

Except the charge had broken off.

It wasn't all that easy tactically to ride up out of the coulee with its sandy footing to attack even a single man when you had to fire from horseback. The Thunder Riders had fallen back to regroup.

Justice thumbed fresh cartridges into his Colt, wiped

the sweat from his eyes, and settled in to wait. Spring Walker had apparently gotten away. That was something. If he had accomplished nothing else on this dismal morning, he had at least saved her life.

Justice watched a deerfly crawl across his bare arm, biting at the drying blood there. He swiped at the fly, chasing it away. It was taking a hell of a long time. Justice had expected the Thunder Riders to come crawling out of the coulee, to fight from their bellies, to close in slowly until a lucky shot got Justice or he ran out of ammunition.

Nothing. The stillness dragged on forever. The grass rustled in the breeze. A gopher snake wove its sinuous way past; two white butterflies tumbled by, performing a mating dance in the air.

The horses rose like a living flesh-and-blood wave from the coulee—and Justice didn't even react. They were riding away. Away from him and back onto the plains, racing away from Wickenburg, returning to the distant hills.

Justice watched them go, smelling their dust, not understanding any of it.

He got to his feet slowly, turning to look across the plains in all directions. His left arm hung limply, his right gripped the Colt revolver. The Thunder Riders were gone.

Then he heard the horses behind him and he peered into the distances, seeing the mounted men coming toward him. Men from Wickenburg?

No, they were wearing blue uniforms. The man in the lead carried a guidon. The soldier beside him was Ray Hardistein. Justice crouched wearily, picked up his gun belt, and strapped it on. Then he holstered his gun and stood waiting. He was too tired to run and there was no place to run to.

It took them fifteen minutes to reach Ruff. The patrol halted as Hardistein lifted his hand. Faces gaped at the torn, bloodied, long-haired scout.

Ray Hardistein came forward, ten feet ahead of the others. "Ruff Justice, I place you under arrest," he said.

Ruff nodded, smiled, and toppled over on his face to lie against the prairie grass.

When he came around again, he was propped up on a bedroll with a blanket over him. His arm had been done up again. It smelled of carbolic disinfectant.

Ray Hardistein was there along with Corporal Bragg, a big-chested, amiable man from Indiana. Bragg was holding a cup of coffee.

"Howdy, Bragg," Justice said.

"Hello, Ruff," Bragg said a little stiffly. He thrust the coffee at Justice, who sat up a little straighter and took it in his hands.

"What's happened here, Ruff?" Ray Hardistein asked. Justice noticed his own gun belt slung over the NCO's shoulder. "There's dead men scattered around. You do it?"

"I did it," Justice said. "Who's the officer here?"

"Me. Acting lieutenant. Everyone else is getting ready for the big one."

"The big one?" Ruff lowered his cup.

"The colonel's going after Fist. The scouts have found his home camp."

"You've got to stop them, Ray."

"Stop them?" Hardistein shrugged. "Can't do that. I've got no reason to try."

"Then get me to the colonel. Now," Justice said, trying to rise.

"I intend to, Ruffin, but even if I tried I couldn't get you back to Lincoln before the colonel takes the field."

"Ray, there's something going on that you know nothing about, that the colonel knows nothing about. Fist doesn't want war; he's been trying to find a way to make peace."

"Couldn't prove it by me," Hardistein said.

"Did the Tinker family make it to Lincoln?"

"Tinker? No. Why? What's happened to them?"

"They were hit by raiders. White raiders. Ray, we've got a pack of white renegades out here who want to make it look like Fist has started a war. Ada Sinclair and a man named Jesse Todd are behind it."

"Ada Sinclair must be pretty far behind it," Ray said cynically. "Since she's dead."

"She's *not* dead." Ruff finally got to his feet with a helping hand from Bragg.

"She better be, they buried her."

"That wasn't Ada Sinclair. Dammit, Ray, listen to me. The women they found murdered was Becky Tandy from the Sternwheeler. Ada and this Todd killed her to make it look like I'd murdered the senator's daughter."

"You've always had an imagination, Justice."

"Yeah," Ruff said bitterly, "I imagine a lot. Those dead men out there are part of this army Ada Sinclair raised. The Indians call them the Thunder Riders. I can show you their camp."

Ray shook his head. "I was sent to look for you, not to follow you all over the country."

"Ray, there's going to be a war—for no reason. You and I have been through a hell of a lot together. You really believe everything they're saying about me?"

"I don't have the privilege of believing or disbelieving," Ray Hardistein said after a long pause. He looked off across the windblown plains. "I'm a soldier, Justice. I got my orders. Bring Ruff Justice in to hang. That's what I intend to do."

13

"You're a soldier," Ruff Justice growled. Hardistein didn't like his tone of voice, but that didn't bother Justice a bit. "You're a soldier and so what if people die for no reason? You know who's going to die first—other soldiers, Ray, the boys from Lincoln. You're a soldier so you'll send your comrades out to die. What's the matter, Ray, afraid I'm going to escape on you? Got those manacles with you? I'll wear them. Tie me to a horse. Put a gun to my head. Dammit all, Ray," Justice said almost desperately, "you've got to do something to stop this. Right now you're the only man on the plains who can."

Bragg had wandered away; now he returned from where a group of soldiers were digging graves for the dead. Ray Hardistein was immobile, staring silently at Ruff Justice.

"Sarge," Bragg said. He jabbed a thumb back over his shoulder. "I just seen a man I know over there."

"Dead?" Ray asked without removing his eyes from Justice.

"Yeah. His name was Vance Hyatt. Came from my part of the country. Man was a stone-cold killer."

"He was, was he?" Ray's eyes narrowed a little more.

"Yeah. Also the boys want to know what to do about the gold these men are carrying. Each of 'em's got somethin' between fifty and two hundred dollars in Philadelphia-mint gold on 'em."

Ruff Justice asked quietly, "What's that sound like to you, Ray?"

"Outlaws maybe."

"Outlaws. That's right. Thunder Riders, Ray." Hardistein looked uncertain and Ruff pressed on. "I know where their camp is, Ray. This morning they were going to attack Wickenburg, but you chased them off. They hit the Watkins place and killed five people. Hit that wagon train at Oregon Folk."

"You can prove that?"

"At their camp I think I can. They've got booty from the Oregon Fork raid. Last night Miss Ada Sinclair was sitting there sipping a little wine they'd taken from a settler's wagon."

"I'm not a lawman, Ruff. It's not my business to track outlaws down."

"Unless their name is Ruff Justice."

"That's not fair."

"Neither is letting people die. We could try the Thunder Riders' camp, Ray. Then maybe the old French fort."

"What in hell is there?"

"The Tinker family, maybe. They were going to start south, but they either didn't make it or didn't try. Maybe one of them was hurt and they decided to sit it out."

"The Tinkers . . ."

"They *know* what happened, Ray. Donna Tinker was held hostage by the Thunder Riders."

"But she escaped."

"She got away, yeah, but she's seen them close up, knows they wear paint and feathers, knows they mean to make a war."

"Justice . . . dammit all. Bragg," Hardistein bellowed, "get those men buried. We're riding."

"To Lincoln, Sarge?"

Ray Hardistein was a long time answering. "West," he said at last. "We're going to see if I can get myself hung beside Mister Justice here."

"Don't worry about that, Ray. I'll hang alone—remember? All they can do to a soldier is shoot him."

"Yeah." Ray managed a small smile. "I must be crazy," he muttered.

"Hell, you'll probably get yourself a shiny medal," Ruff said. "Got a horse?"

"And the manacles?" Ray asked.

"I said I'd wear 'em if you wanted me to."

"Ah, Christ, Justice . . . Trooper, get Mister Justice a horse!"

The one he ended up on was a captured Thunder Rider's mount, a high-stepping, feisty blue roan. Ruff sat the horse's back as Ray organized his men, briefing them quickly. Justice looked up the coulee and down, but there was no sign of Spring Walker. It was just as well. Wherever she was, she would be safer than she would be returning to the Thunder Riders' camp . . . unless she had gone back to Fist's village. Colonel MacEnroe was riding that way with plenty of support, and as far as the colonel or any other man there knew, Fist was ready and willing to make violent war.

Justice thought of the lady behind this, of the cool blonde with the bright-green eyes and the bloody heart. "Damn you, Ada Sinclair, " he said softly, "damn you to a cold and haunted hell."

"Talking to yourself?" Ray Hardistein asked, riding up beside Justice.

"Throwing curses to the wind."

"Throw a few for me," Hardistein said. "How far is this camp, Justice?"

"Twenty miles or so."

"Then let's get riding, Ruff. Before I can change my

mind. Dammit all, you're a troublesome man to have for a friend!"

Ruff grinned and started down the coulee on the blue roan. Riding hurt, but there was no help for that. His arm didn't seem to be getting any better no matter who worked on it.

The sky grew pale and clear but the wind never abated. They worked their way westward throughout the day, Ray Hardistein remaining grim and silent.

There were only a few hours of daylight left when they emerged from the trees and sat looking down at the camp of the Thunder Riders.

"See anyone?" Ray asked, easing his horse up beside Ruff's.

"Looks deserted."

"No smoke. Nothing. You sure this is the place, Ruffin?"

Justice answered soberly, "I should be. Go on down and have a look?"

"I suppose." Hardistein shifted in his saddle and summoned Bragg. "Keep half the men in these trees. Rifles at the ready. I don't know what we've got here." The look he gave Justice indicated that he thought it might just be a tall tale. "All right, Ruff, let's see what the camp of these Thunder Riders looks like."

They rode slowly down out of the pines and into the camp, splashing across the little creek. They could see nothing, hear nothing.

One of the soldiers said, "Just an old mining camp, Sarge."

Ray glanced at Justice but said nothing. It was obvious the NCO had his doubts, and Ruff couldn't blame him. The camp looked as if it had been deserted for years, but then it had looked that way when it was full of people: like a ghost town stumbled upon by accident.

They swung down in the middle of the muddy street,

Justice leading the way to the store. It was there that he hoped to find something to prove the truth of his story.

Hardistein walked behind him, hand on his service revolver. "Tell your people to water their horses at the stream, Ray, not to just use any water barrels they find."

"I'll tell them later," Ray said. "Let's look inside."

Ruff nodded, tried the door, and found it locked. He kicked it open and went in. It was all there. Guns, supplies, food. He looked at Ray, who was still without expression.

"This doesn't prove much, Ruff."

"We'll find enough to prove it," Justice promised. He crossed to the store counter, slid across it, and began rummaging around. A small tin box was hidden there and he hefted it to the counter. Ray took a look inside while three of his troopers searched the rest of the store.

Inside the tin box was a bible, a picture of a baby, two gold rings. The names in the bible were Emma and Roger Saxon.

"The Oregon Fork massacre, Ray," Justice said. "Loot from that."

"You know these people?"

"No."

"Neither did I. This stuff could have come from anywhere." Ray dropped the articles back into the box.

"Sarge?" The trooper came forward carrying a lady's mantle. "This mean anything?"

"That's Ada Sinclair's, Ray. She was wearing it last night."

"It is, is it?" Ray took the cloak and spread it on the counter. Justice's finger fell on the embroidered initials inside. "A.S."

"That still doesn't—" Then Ray himself found the letter folded up in the pocket of the cloak, left behind to dry by Ada Sinclair. He unfolded it carefully and read it aloud.

Dear Miss Sinclair,

Everything is organized here. Tell the people back East we are open for business. There's a snag or two we'll discuss when you arrive with your father. Nothing to worry about. We need more payroll, though.

It was signed Jesse Todd.

Ray tipped his hat back, took in a slow breath as if it were painful to do so, and shook his head. "It doesn't prove much, Ruff. That letter could be explained away."

"No, one thing doesn't prove much, Ray, but take it all together. It smells, doesn't it?"

"It does, but—"

"What's all *this* about, Sarge?" another soldier asked, and as Ray turned, the trooper unloaded his arms on the counter. Buckskin shirts, headbands, feathers, even a dark wig, a jar of paint, bracelets, and a war ax.

Ray fingered the items, looked at Ruff, and nodded. "Sorry, Justice."

"Why? Don't waste the time on being sorry, Ray. Let's just catch up with those bastards and stop this war."

"You make it sound simple, Justice. How many men did you say they had?"

"Between fifty and sixty now."

"I've got a twelve-man patrol, Ruff. If you ask me, the smart thing to do now is try to get through to Colonel MacEnroe. He'll be pulling out at dawn."

"That's fifty miles, Ray!"

"Yes," the sergeant admitted, "it is. We'll try to intercept MacEnroe along his line of travel."

"And if you miss him?"

"We've got big trouble. What else is there to do?"

"Move the Cheyenne," Ruff said quietly.

"Do what? Ride into Fist's camp and tell him to get out of the way before our army butchers him? I'd really shine in the colonel's eyes with that stunt. Sounds more like something Ruff Justice would pull."

"That's what I intended," Ruff answered. He smiled at Ray. "Fist wouldn't like seeing any bluecoats around anyway. It'll have to be me."

"You look like you've got a fast ride in you," Ray said, examining the exhausted, bloody scout.

"I'll try it."

"And he'll listen to you, will he?"

"Not likely," Ruff had to reply. "He wants peace, but I figure if he's attacked, he'll stand and fight."

"But you're going to convince him otherwise. You must be a great friend of his, Ruffin."

"Sure," Ruff said, "great enough that I'll be surprised if he doesn't kill me the next time I see him."

"I don't like it, any of it." Ray looked again at the handfuls of beads and feathers, Indian attire that had been piled on the counter. "But I can't see that we've got any choice."

"Then let's get to it. We don't have any time at all to waste."

"The men are going to be thrilled with a night ride."

"They'll be even less thrilled if this war opens up, Ray, and that's what is going to happen if you can't cut off MacEnroe."

"All right, Ruffin. The Thunder Riders . . . where do you figure they are now?"

"I don't know, but watch yourself. They've plenty of guns and ammunition, and it might just suit their purposes to leave a massacred army patrol on the plains."

"Yeah." Ray Hardistein dropped the string of beads he had been holding. "And maybe it would suit their purposes to chop up a pain-in-the-ass army scout. You watch yourself, Ruff. Luck to you."

"Luck to you, Ray." He looked again at the counter in the Thunder Rider's store. "You might want to take that bible and the picture along. Someone would likely want them."

Outside, it was cold, the wind quick. Ruff had taken a heavy twill coat from the store, but it didn't do much to keep him warm. He had a borrowed black hat pulled tightly down, a Winchester rifle, and a Colt revolver strapped on. The weapons didn't help to instill a sense of confidence in the scout. They weren't enough against the Thunder Riders and they were less than useless against Fist if the Cheyenne war leader decided that he had no more reason to let Ruff Justice live.

And it might just happen that way. If Fist found out that the white army was massed to attack him, he might just let his dream of peace be blown away by the Dakota winds.

Justice swung aboard the blue roan and looked back once at the camp. Ray had taken the time to torch it and now fire exploded from windows and raced through the flimsy tents, sending towering clouds of smoke into the night sky. When the fire was out, the plains would be a little cleaner.

Justice started on, urging the roan southward, westward toward the broken hills. There, the Cheyenne warlord was still dreaming his dream of an honorable peace while the great army of retribution slept, readying itself to fight.

"Luck to you, Ray," Justice said under his breath. If Hardistein couldn't cut MacEnroe's column off, there was just nothing to stop this war, nothing at all.

Ruff lifted his horse into a canter and set his eyes on a southern constellation. He rode swiftly but cautiously. He hadn't forgotten for a minute.

The Thunder Riders were still out there somewhere, and with a sudden sinking sensation Justice realized where they must be headed.

Southward, westward. Toward Fist's camp. They would

want to be there when it started. They could ride in with the soldiers, a great civilian army volunteering to do their duty. They could ride in and do their killing with impunity, and to all the world they would seem like heroes, their fair-haired, lovely leader a public benefactress.

Her father's own dream of peace would sleep with Fist's, sleep in the ashes of the burned Cheyenne village, sleep alongside their dead.

Ruff lashed the roan savagely and the startled horse began to run, to run hard across the night-cloaked Dakota plains.

14

The old French fort stood stolid, decrepit, nearly featureless in the clearing among the pines. The brush had long ago grown up there, purple sage and sumac, and now the pines were making a comeback. Nothing lasts long.

The Indians had burned half of the fort, torn down most of the palisade, but a few yards of wall, a blockhouse, scorched by fire, and a stone warehouse still stood.

The Tinker family waited there, waited forever. The Thunder Riders had caught up with them.

Justice stood in stony silence, looking at the bodies. Donna Tinker, her mother, her father, and two brothers. Ruff had tried to save them, but he had only sent them to their deaths. They could have told the truth and so they had to be found, and when they were found Tate Hawkins and his men had brutally murdered them—for a few gold dollars.

It was then that real anger began to build inside Justice, a fiery, killing anger that made him want to take the Thunder Riders, one by one and see that the same was done to them. Slowly, methodically, heartlessly.

"By God if I get the chance . . ." But he wasn't able to hold the pure hatred of the moment, to descend to that savagery of the heart. But they would pay—if Bismarck had to build the greatest scaffold ever constructed and hang fifty men at a time on it, they would pay—or Ruff Justice would spend the rest of his days tracking them down.

There wasn't time to bury the dead. He swung aboard the roan and went on, winding through the clean pines, listening to the jays and chattering squirrels.

The Tinkers hadn't gotten through. Ruff had still held out a hope that they could have reached Lincoln with the truth about the Thunder Riders. That left only the slender chance that Ray Hardistein's patrol could intercept MacEnroe on his march and the even more slender chance that Ruff could talk a man of pride, a man of war, into running from the soldiers.

Smoke rose in a thin, wavering shaft from beyond the hills. Ruff felt his heart slow a little. Not yet—they hadn't hit Fist's camp yet. The Indians were still going about their business: cooking, hunting, fishing in the nearby river.

Ruff urged the roan on faster yet. The horse stumbled once with exhaustion and Ruff yanked its head up. They went down the pine-clad slope rapidly and crossed the river, surprising several Indian women who were doing their wash there.

They scurried away as Justice rode on through the trees and into the heart of the Cheyenne camp. Alone, uninvited.

He walked the weary horse toward the yellow tepee of the Cheyenne leader, having no idea what to expect. His spirits got an unexpected lift when Spring Walker emerged from another tent and came toward him on the run.

Ruff swung down and stood waiting for her. Spring Walker threw herself against his chest, hugging his neck, kissing him.

"I thought you were dead, thought they would kill you."

"I got a reprieve," Ruff said. "I don't know how long it will last. I've got to talk to Fist."

"Of peace?" she asked hopefully.

"Of war," Ruff answered, and the hope fell away from Spring Walker's face.

"The Thunder Riders?" she asked.

"Afraid not. Not just them anyway. I have to talk to Fist. It's urgent."

"He may not wish to speak to you."

"Maybe not, but he's dreamed of peace—for the good of his people. If he's still thinking of the good of his people, he'll want to talk to me." Although he wouldn't much want to hear what Justice was going to suggest.

Spring Walker's hand lingered on Ruff's arm for a moment longer and then fell away. She looked toward Fist's tepee with doubt.

"I will see, then," she said, taking resolve. She turned and marched to the lodge of the war leader. It seemed that Spring Walker was in there a long time, a hell of a long time. Curious Cheyenne walked past, studying Justice, and kids played dust-raising games through the camp, their dogs yapping excitedly.

Spring Walker finally emerged again and she nodded. "He will see you, but his mood is dark, Ruff Justice."

"So's mine," was Justice's reply, and he marched into the tepee where Fist waited for him.

The Cheyenne leader's mood was indeed dark. He glared at Ruff. "I did not think you would return."

"I had to, Fist."

"You have seen the white war leaders?"

"No," Justice answered.

The Cheyenne said, "Then you have failed me."

"In a way, yes. I just don't want you to fail your people, Fist."

"What do you mean?" Fist came nearer. Bare-chested, scarred, black eyes glowing.

"I don't want you to let them get killed. You've dreamed of peace. You had a plan to bring peace, but it didn't work. Now you have a way of finding that peace."

"How?" Fist asked warily.

"By leaving this camp, by running," Justice told him outright.

"Running!" Fist laughed scornfully. "Who would I run from, the Thunder Riders, the army? You know I will not run, Justice. Why have you come here with this idea?"

Briefly, Ruff told him. Told him that the army was on the way, that Ray Hardistein was trying to cut them off, that the Thunder Riders were waiting out there somewhere—to join the battle, he thought. Fist listened in sullen silence, taking it all in, not commenting until Justice had finished the entire tale.

"If you would bring me this story and then tell me to run, Ruff Justice, you do not know Fist. I am a warrior first, and a peacemaker when it seems I must be. I am not a coward. Never a coward."

"It's not cowardly to let your people live, Fist. It's only right. This can be stopped, but until it is, it makes sense for you to put yourself out of the army's way."

"Never!"

"Then you will all die."

"And so will the whites," Fist promised.

"What in hell are you gaining that way, Fist? What?"

Through the tent flap a half-naked boy of three entered. He walked to Fist, thrust out dirty, pudgy arms, and was picked up by the war leader. The boy clung to Fist's neck and from time to time peered shyly at Justice.

"The little ones will also be punished, Fist," Ruff said quietly. "They will suffer too. For what? For a warrior's pride?"

"Get out," Fist said, and his voice seemed to have shrunken, contracting deep in his throat. "Get out of my home. Let me think, let me discover inside me what I must do, Ruff Justice. Go now!"

Ruff turned sharply and ducked out of the tent. It was cool and bright outside. Spring Walker stood waiting for him. She walked to him and took his arm without saying a word.

Two crows sailed high in the flawless blue sky. The wind whispered through the stand of mature pines. Somewhere on the prairie, out of sight, out of hearing, death approached. How much time did they have? How long would Fist take to make his decision?

The Cheyenne had assembled as if summoned by Fist, though no one had said a word. They stood with their blankets around them, stoic, patient.

When Fist emerged, he wore a scarlet shirt, scarlet headband, buckskin pants, breechclout, and a bear-claw necklace. In his hand was a rifle.

His eyes went first to Ruff Justice—a quick, electric glance—and then lifted to his people.

"Strike the camp, we are leaving."

"Leaving?" one warrior asked, but a gesture from Fist cut off that question and any others that might have followed.

"Strike the camp now. We are moving."

"You won't be sorry, Fist," Ruff Justice said as the Indians hurried away to begin moving.

"I am already sorry, Ruff Justice. Sorry in my heart for my lost warrior's pride."

"You're doing this for your people."

"Yes. For the people. Why are you standing there, Spring Walker? Can you do nothing to help?" Fist lashed out.

"I am going," she said. She touched Ruff's arm and scurried away into the bedlam of the camp. How many times had the Cheyenne broken camp in this way, at first following the roaming buffalo herds, fleeing hard winters in the north, and later traveling out of the path of the approaching white settlers and soldiers?

"Where are we going?" Ruff asked.

"We?" Fist studied the scout's face with irritation. "To the caves," he said finally. "Along the river. You know these caves, Ruff Justice?"

"I know them—not well, but I know them."

"They will not find us there, I think. If they do, they will never take us from them."

"If we—" Ruff was interrupted by an incoming rider, a slender Cheyenne brave of twenty or so. His spotted horse was lathered, his eyes wide.

"They are coming, Fist!" The eyes of the young man flashed briefly to Ruff's white face. "Soldiers, many soldiers. A long column of them by the Butterfly Rock."

"Your soldier friend did not stop the colonel."

"He may not have had time," Ruff answered.

"Perhaps they will not be stopped at all. Perhaps your soldier friend did not intend to stop them."

"Ray would have stopped them if he could. Give me a fresh horse, Fist," Justice said, taking a step forward to stand before the shorter, broader Indian. "I'll stop them myself."

"They will shoot you."

"Maybe so," Justice answered, "but I'll stop them anyway—if they'll listen to me."

Fist thought it over. "No. I will not let you go."

"Why not?"

"You know now where we are going. You could guide the soldiers to the caves."

"Fist, dammit all, I'm on your side in this. I'll give you my word. You said my word was good, remember? You said you could trust Ruff Justice when he spoke."

"No." Fist shook his head. "Not now. I cannot take this risk. You are coming with us."

Then he turned and said something so rapidly in his own

tongue to the younger warrior that Ruff couldn't follow it. He only caught the words, "Make ready."

"Fist, you can't fight them."

Fist's eyes had hardened. "If they will fight, then we must."

"All right," Justice said with resignation, "but let's give Ray Hardistein time to intercept the column. Let's proceed to the caves and wait. Maybe we can outrun this war."

The Cheyenne were nearly ready to ride. The tepees had been left standing, most of their utensils left behind. They had only their children, their blankets, and their guns.

Fist lifted a clenched hand and they started away, northward toward the caves along the river.

Ruff tried once more, "Let me ride to the cavalry column, Fist."

"You may ride with us as a friend, Ruff Justice," Fist said. "Or you may try to leave. If you do that, I shall have you killed."

Fist's horse had been brought around and he swung aboard it smoothly, holding his rifle high in a signal to his warriors. The Cheyenne leader looked at Ruff one last time, a warning glance, and rode out, heeling his pony hard to reach the head of his line of people.

Spring Walker was there, leading Ruff's worn-out blue roan. She handed him the reins and Justice swung up. She could see it in his eyes and she asked him, "You are not thinking of defying Fist?"

"I could reach that column, MacEnroe might listen to me—long enough to talk to Fist anyway. Maybe I could delay them until Hardistein arrives."

"Fist said you must not go," Spring Walker said in an urgent whisper. "Look!"

Ruff looked and what he saw cooled any thought of trying to reach MacEnroe. Three warriors sat their horses watching him, all were armed. The only way to reach the cavalry was over the dead bodies of those three.

Ruff cursed under his breath and with a last look eastward, to where the unseen army was making its slow way toward the Cheyenne camp, he rode out with Spring Walker, the three guards behind him.

"The army, how long will it take them to arrive?" Spring Walker asked.

"From Butterfly? Three hours maybe."

"By then we will be well hidden," Spring Walker said with confidence.

"They'll track us. A party this size—they'll track us." Shay could track a party of this size with his horse at a dead run. The rain of a few days before would have been welcome now, a hard-driving rain to erase their tracks, but the sky was clear as crystal, the sun sharp and hard like a demonic yellow eye following the Cheyenne northward.

The caves were ahead, along the huge red bluffs. The Cheyenne would be safe there—for a time. Shay would track them down eventually. And although it was a monumental task for the cavalry to root Fist out of those caves, MacEnroe would do it if he had set his mind to it. If Ray hadn't stopped him, if the Thunder Riders hadn't reached his detachment and slaughtered them.

The caves, Ruff Justice reflected, would make suitable tombs for a people.

They broke out of the pines and emerged near the narrow trail Spring Walker had shown Ruff earlier, the trail that slithered down the face of the bluff toward the honeycomb caves below.

The Cheyenne had started down the trail already, those afoot first, women carrying children, the old hurrying the best way they could. Then came the warriors, flint-eyed, willing to run but ready to fight.

In another minute they had their fight. The guns opened up from the far side of the river and a woman screamed in terror as she was hit by the first volley of bullets. She fell from the trail, cartwheeling toward the river, far, far below.

"Soldiers," someone yelled, "the soldiers have come!"

But it wasn't soldiers. It was the Thunder Riders and they had the Cheyenne just where they wanted them, where they could kill every last member of Fist's band and finish the war that the cold-eyed, too-beautiful blond woman had begun.

15

Ruff Justice swung down, letting the reins to the roan slip through his fingers as the horse reared away. Dropping to one knee, he answered the fire from across the gorge with his Winchester repeater.

There wasn't much to shoot at but smoke, maybe he could at least keep a few heads down. On the trail below, another woman was shot, dragged away by friends. A warrior fifteen feet from Ruff had the top of his head ripped away by a bullet from the Thunder Riders' guns.

"Justice!" Spring Walker yelled his name three times before he heard her. His cheek was pressed to the walnut stock of the repeater, his attention on the smoke from the distant guns as he levered through round after round, the bellow of the .44-.40 in his ears.

He turned his eyes finally to the Cheyenne woman, who pleaded with him, "What can we do? Where can we run?"

"Get to the caves!"

"Down the trail?"

"It's that or face the cavalry. Get going, now."

The Cheyenne guns had taken up the battle now, answering the withering fire from across the gorge with their own. The gorge was filled with powder smoke, with the cries of the injured.

Fist led his people on, his warriors covering the advance from the bluff. The Thunder Riders had it their own way for a time, but the Cheyenne warriors' firepower began to tell. Most of those who had been trapped on the path were able to make their way to the waiting caves below under the protection of the Indian rifles.

"Justice!" Spring Walker was still there beside him, and Ruff snarled at her.

"Get down the trail!"

"Not without you."

In another moment there was no choice. The Thunder Riders appeared from out of the pines, charging on horseback toward the Indians still remaining on the bluff. It was a well-planned attack, but the timing was off just enough to defeat the pincer movement.

Todd had wanted the men behind the Indians to close in as the guns from across the gorge held the Cheyenne back. But these men weren't soldiers and they had missed by just enough to allow most of the Indians to slip through unharmed.

Justice spun as the first of the Thunder Riders opened up from behind, and his rifle took only seconds to cut down two men.

A bullet into the face of a rider turned his head into a mask of blood, blowing him from his horse's back. A second rider took a slug from the Winchester in the chest.

Ruff missed a shot, heard the thud of a bullet as it impacted into the earth beside his knee, and fired again, hitting a sorrel horse in the chest. The horse folded up and the rider flew into the air, the somersaulting sorrel crushing him.

Ruff started working his way toward the path. A dozen Cheyenne fought beside him, firing at the Thunder Riders, turning the mounted attack.

From across the gorge sporadic fire continued as Justice and Spring Walker, afoot, reached the trail and dashed madly down it. Bullets whined off the face of the red bluff, pursuing them with the promise of sudden death.

Ruff reached the first cave with a headlong dive as bullets rang after him into the cavern, where a dozen Cheyenne fired back at the snipers across the gorge.

Spring Walker was behind him. She slipped and went down flat on her belly. Ruff grabbed an arm and dragged her in. The guns fired for another ten minutes, became a sporadic sharpshooting contest, and then halted.

The wind sang up the long gorge. Ruff could hear the river running in the stillness. Now and then a wounded Cheyenne groaned with pain.

Ruff rose, reloaded his gun, and stood looking down at the gorge. He could see no movement across the way, no splash of color. They might have been attacked by the canyon ghosts for all the signs of living human beings out there.

Fist was there and he made his way heavily toward Justice. There was anger in the Cheyenne's eyes and a hatred Ruff hadn't seen before. He held his rifle tightly with both hands, as if he were going to club Justice with it. Ruff waited, his eyes expressionless.

"This is the end. Now we are finished, Ruff Justice. Finished to the last of my band."

"I don't get you. Those men over there? They can't get to us."

"They are *white*, Justice! Don't you see that? They are white and we have killed some of them, made a battle with them. Now, when the soldiers come, there will be two armies out there. Now the soldiers will find evidence of our wish for war."

"It's not going to work that way," Ruff Justice said soberly. His blue eyes were cold, meeting Fist's evenly.

"And who is going to stop it all? Who is going to kill the Thunder Riders, who is going to stop the army, who is going to tell the truth about this?"

"Me." Ruff Justice was still looking Fist dead in the eye. He saw the bitterness, the frustration and cold anger there. "I'm going to do it, Fist. I swear to you I'll stop them."

"Alone?" Fist laughed.

"Alone. That's the way it has to be."

"Will you tell me how you are going to do this, Ruff Justice? Tell me how you are going to emerge from this cave, let alone kill all the Thunder Riders? How you are going to stop the army, how you are going to have the whites believe us and not their own kind?"

Ruff didn't answer the Cheyenne leader. What in hell could he say? He didn't know how he was going to do it; he only knew that if there was a way, he was going to try it.

He asked, "I suppose you'll let me leave now? The whites know where you are anyway."

"Leave, leave," Fist said, waving a hand in frustration. "Go where you want, do what you will. I must prepare my people to die. There is no way out of this cave for us, no way to escape slaughter."

Fist stalked away, fury evident in each movement of his body. A woman groaned and Fist started in that direction, taking a minute to crouch beside her and stroke her forehead.

"He feels he has failed his people, Ruff Justice," Spring Walker said.

"I know he does." Ruff felt the same way—as though he too had failed the Cheyenne. What he could have done differently he didn't know, but that didn't dissipate the unhappy feeling.

"What you told Fist—that you were going to fight alone," Spring Walker said, standing close to the tall man, "you said that out of passion."

"Out of passion," Ruff agreed.

"Since nothing can be done . . ."

"But I meant it. I'll do something," Justice said. "Fist and I are the same in that respect. To sit and do nothing when we'd rather be fighting, rather die fighting than just take it, well, that's something that galls a man."

"When there *is* something to be done," Spring Walker said excitedly. Now she held the sleeves to Ruff's coat, looking up at him with astonishment. "But what can Fist do? It is suicide to try to attack from out of this cave, down that trail. It is suicide for you to go out alone. There *is* nothing to do, Ruff Justice. Nothing at all."

"We'll see," Ruff answered tightly. "We'll see about that."

A bullet, and then half a dozen more were fired into the cave by snipers across the way. Ruff led Spring Walker away from the cavern's mouth.

"After dark," he told her, "I'm going out."

"After dark," she repeated blankly.

"I want you to find me a rope. Someone must have one. As long a one as you can turn up."

"Yes," she said, "I will find you a rope. Justice, you are going out to die."

"Very likely," he answered frankly.

"Then we will not sleep together anymore. Will you sleep with me now?"

"Here—?"

"I know another place. A little cave. There is a tunnel to it. No one will bother us." Her voice grew more excited, her eyes brighter. She was frightened and hungry at the same time. "I will get a buffalo robe and lie with you, and in a hundred years I will remember that we have slept together."

Justice looked at her a long while before he nodded slightly. Spring Walker turned and went to get her buffalo robe. Ruff watched and waited.

Inside, Fist held a glum, low-voiced conference with some of his lieutenants while women held their children, rocking them, singing softly. In the mouth of the cave, framed against the coloring sky, half a dozen warriors stood watch.

Beyond the mouth of the cave death watched back, waiting for its time to come. Where was MacEnroe? He had been too far off to hear the shots, but he must have found Fist's camp by now—unless Ray had cut him off, turned him back. That would be the final irony.

"Ruff Justice?"

Her voice was soft, her mouth showing both expectation and sadness. She had her buffalo robe across her arm, and as Justice turned, she took his hand, leading him across the cavern past dark expressionless eyes to a smaller cave and then to a tunnel.

Entering that, they were lost in darkness. Spring Walker ducked low and crept on. Ruff put a hand on her hip and followed. The world had gone still and silent and black.

"Here," Spring Walker said breathily, and there was a moment while she spread the buffalo robe, another while she slipped from her dress and waited for Justice to remove his clothes.

He went down to her, finding her soft and warm and eager for him.

"You see, no gun." She laughed, taking Ruff's hand, rubbing it across her body, down over her full, firm breasts to her long, sleek thighs and between them to the thatch of dark hair and the warmth beneath it.

Ruff lay down beside her, leaving his hand between her legs, touching her gently, sparking a response in the Cheyenne girl. She rolled to him, her arms going around his neck, her lips touching his face on the mouth, cheeks, eyes.

"The rope . . ." Ruff started to say.

"I have it," she said, putting a finger to his lips. "Now say no more about tonight, the next hour, but only live this minute with me."

Her hand groped for his lengthening shaft and found it. Spring Walker lifted her leg, throwing it across Ruff's, and slipped him into position. With a long slow thrust Justice settled deeply into her, feeling Spring Walker shudder as she clung to him, her breasts flattened against his chest, her lips whispering soft, meaningless words in his ears.

Ruff's hand slid behind her and drew her closer, holding her tightly against him, gripping her hard buttocks tightly, fingers digging into the flesh as he swayed against her.

His head lowered to her breasts and lost itself between them. He kissed the inner curve of her breasts, then sought the taut dark nipples eagerly. Spring Walker stroked his head and swayed against him.

For a minute they were still, lying side by side in the darkness of the cave, Ruff feeling the slow throbbing in his loins as Spring Walker's fingers touched his shaft where he entered her, traced patterns across his sack.

Her breath was shallow and quick, and she began to budge Ruff with her pelvis, to open and grow damper still. She rolled onto her back, Ruff following her, and lifted her legs high. Ruff knelt before her, his fingers toying with the small, erect tab of flesh at the juncture of her thighs until Spring Walker gasped and pulled him down to her, her legs locking around his waist.

She ground herself against him, a slow, heavy, circular motion as she nipped at his shoulders and chest with her sharp white teeth.

Ruff moved slowly against her, letting her take her time until, with a frenzied, sudden series of movements, she reached a hard climax, thrashing in Ruff's arms, her head rolling from side to side, body and hands clutching at him, lifting Justice to his own jolting completion.

The world went silent and still again. She lay beneath him, her hands stroking his back, gripping his shoulders.

Then she was still, only her soft, heated breathing breaking the silence, and for a little while Ruff Justice slept.

He was awakened by the girl crouched over him. Spring Walker shook his shoulder and said, "It is dark." Her voice was toneless, slightly savage.

Ruff sat up, staring at the darkness. He could barely make out Spring Walker's silhouette. Her body was set into sharp angles.

"I've got to do it, woman," Ruff said, reaching for her.

"I said nothing," she answered, growing snappish. Ruff's hand was on her arm but she might have been a hundred miles away.

"You didn't have to say anything."

"A warrior must go to battle. A woman must stay behind," Spring Walker recited.

"All right, then, you understand."

Ruff sat up, searched around for his clothing, and began dressing in the darkness. Spring Walker never moved. She remained crouched beside him, staring at nothing.

"The rope," Ruff prompted, and she pressed a coil of hemp into his hand. He was on his knees, rifle in hand now, and he started to kiss her cheek but she pulled away.

"Go now. Go and die."

There was no point in trying to say anything else to the woman. Justice worked his way out of the tunnel into the main cavern where the Cheyenne waited for their last battle. The only light in the cave came from the glimmering blue stars outside.

Ruff found Fist near the mouth of the cave. The Cheyenne leader turned to study Ruff, noting the rifle in his hand, the belt gun, the coil of rope over his shoulder. Justice had shed the heavy borrowed coat he had worn and now he shivered a little in the darkness.

"Anything happening out there?" Ruff wanted to know.

Fist answered with a slow shake of his head. "Nothing."

"No sign of the soldiers?"

"Not yet," Fist answered, "but they will come."

"I'm not so sure now. Maybe they were turned back," Ruff suggested.

"And so we must die before the guns of the Thunder Riders and not those of the bluecoats," Fist said stonily.

"Maybe." Ruff was studying the night, the bluffs opposite, the river that ran wide and shallow through the gorge itself. "Maybe we can stop it all still, Fist."

"You are going out there?"

Ruff answered, "I'm going out. If there's a chance to do anything."

"There is no chance."

"Then," Ruff said with a grin, "I'm going anyway."

"Why?" Fist was genuinely puzzled. "Why are you doing this, Justice? There is nothing to be gained by it. Slip away, go back and live with the Crow again. One man can go where he likes on a night like this if he is a warrior like me, like you."

"And run out on my friends?" Ruff asked.

"Friends?" Fist tasted the word and found it bitter. "How can we be friends, Ruff Justice?"

"How can we not if we're going to survive out here? These others, these Thunder Riders, they don't want a peace, don't want a single white to be friends with a single Indian. We can destroy them, Fist, we can break their filthy little plan. We can be friends."

Fist turned half away. "Go if you are going to go, Ruff Justice. Do not speak of friendship. Just go."

Ruff shifted his rifle, looked again to the night beyond the cavern mouth, again at Fist and the slender Indian woman who stood in the back of the cave, arms folded beneath her breasts.

And then he went. Into the dark hell beyond the cave, into the sights of the Thunder Riders.

16

Ruff Justice ducked out of the cave and onto the sloping narrow trail. Crouching, he waited, watching the night-darkened bluffs around him. He could see nothing, hear nothing but the river and chorusing frogs, but he could feel it.

There was danger, death, anger, and terror floating on the night breeze. Still he waited, seeing no sign of a fire. The Thunder Riders were being cautious now; for the first time they faced an enemy willing to fight back, capable of doing so with deadly precision. They had Fist boxed in, but they didn't have him beaten just yet.

There would be sentries on the bluff above Ruff, more sentries at the head and foot of the trail. Tate Hawkins wasn't much of a man, but he wasn't a bad general. He knew how to kill.

Ruff was left with one way down from the trail: over the side on the rope Spring Walker had found for him. Now, rising, he lashed the rope to a projecting, solid knob of red granite. Testing it, he was satisfied that it could take his weight.

A length of rope off the end of the coil formed a sling for his Winchester, which Justice slipped across his neck and shoulder before taking the rope in his hand. He peered down into the gorge, at the star-silvered river far below, and began the long climb down.

The wind tugged at Justice and shifted his body as he dangled from the rope, working his way down the face of the rugged bluff. A sudden gust twisted him around so that his back was to the wall of stone behind him. The river seemed impossibly distant; the trail above him had vanished into the night.

His wounded arm ached like the devil. His hands burned as he let the rope slip through them. Sweat stood out coldly on Ruff's forehead, trickling into his eyes to sting them. There was nothing he could do to wipe it away.

He could do nothing at all but continue his descent, hoping that some sharp-eyed Thunder Rider didn't pick him out from the dark background and open up with a repeating rifle.

It was fifteen minutes later—fifteen minutes that seemed like days—before he touched the floor of the canyon, the gravel and sand pushed out of the river bottom by the constant river.

Ruff unslung his rifle and crouched for long minutes, leaning against the wall of the canyon, taking in deep, revitalizing breaths of cold air. His shoulder throbbed, his hands were raw. The river presented a shifting kaleidoscope of black and silver, running past over gigantic boulders.

Then Ruff saw the fire.

They had planned well. From above no fire was visible. "Inside a cave," Ruff guessed. He watched it for a time, the distant, dully glowing reddish thing wavering in the night breeze. They were there. What he could do against them he didn't know. It was madness to attack the large body of men Hawkins and Todd had assembled, but there was nothing else to be done.

And so he would attack.

Ruff Justice walked to the edge of the river, watching it

froth and flow. He wasn't going to wade through that. As shallow as the river ran, it ran swiftly. A horse would have a hard time of it; a man afoot had no chance at all.

That meant he was going swimming.

Icy and quick, the river discouraged such ideas, but he had to do it. Ruff found what he wanted: a twisted snag, the remains of an ancient cottonwood tree, or the top of it.

He grappled with it, tugged it to the edge of the water, lifted his rifle high into the broken branches, and shoved off. The tree bobbed deeply and then darted away, drifting downstream on the rapid current with Justice kicking his feet, trying to force the snag toward the far shore.

The water bit at his flesh with iron cold teeth. The current yanked him, twisting Ruff and his vessel one way and then the other sharply. The tree came up against a huge boulder and the air was knocked from Justice's lungs as he nearly lost his grip.

He looked up, saw the fire, and was carried along.

The snag slowed, passing through a heavily moving vortex that had trapped other branches and debris. Justice was nearly in the center of the river. He could see the fire clearly above him, hear drifting, muted voices. The whirlpool refused to release him. Someone came to the mouth of the cave and stood staring at the river. Ruff pressed his head against the trunk of the cottonwood and held on, the cold water swirling around him.

"What're you doing, Jake?" a voice asked. It was easily recognizable. You didn't hear Deke Connely speak and forget how it sounded easily. Justice had assumed Spring Walker's arrow had killed him, but Deke or his twin was up there in the firelit cave.

The man he was talking to had raised a rifle to his shoulder, sighting down it directly toward Justice. Ruff watched him with one eye, kicking his feet below the surface of the water, trying to break the hold the whirlpool had on his primitive craft.

''Thought I seen somebody,'' Jake answered.

''You see Indians everywhere—bad as old Cy Benjamin.'' Deke growled, ''Put the gun up and sit down.''

''I'm telling you, Deke!''

Ruff's frantic efforts had finally forced the cottonwood limb up and out of the trough, and he drifted away as Deke Connely stumped forward to join his fellow soldier. It was Deke all right; that grizzly bear body of his was unmistakable. His bare torso was swathed in bandages.

''Where?'' Deke demanded.

The man with him turned again and opened up with his rifle, blasting apart a stack of driftwood that had been caught in the whirlpool's tenacious grip.

''Fool,'' Deke Connely grunted, and that was the last word Ruff heard as he drifted on, nearing the shore. Above him other caves showed light and movement now. The Thunder Riders had entrenched themselves well.

Ruff paddled toward the shore, ducking again quickly as he spotted someone posted on the beach. The guard was walking slowly up and down, hat pulled low, rifle over his shoulder military-style.

The cottonwood branch nudged the shore and swung around, and the guard glanced that way uneasily. He took a few hesitant steps in Ruff's direction and then seemed to lose interest.

Ruff let out his breath and his grip on his rifle slackened a little. The guard turned his back and paced slowly away through the darkness. Ruff drew silently close to the shore, lifted himself out of the river, and darted toward the dark, head-high willows that crowded the bluff.

In the willows he crouched, checking his weapons, his eyes flickering from point to point, alert to any approaching danger. The guard on the beach wasn't as alert.

He had his shoulders hunched, his head down as he strode along the sandy shore, the river's muffled roar in his ears. The guard never saw the man in buckskins rise up and slash across his throat with the razor-edged bowie knife. All he felt was the sudden shock of pain, the rapid descent into the unending darkness.

Ruff stepped away from the blood-smeared body, looked around, and dragged it into the willows. Emerging, he worked his way northward, keeping to the shadows cast by the bluffs. The stars seemed large, glaring in a blue-black sky.

The second guard was asleep when Ruff nearly stumbled over him. His head jerked up and Ruff kicked him in the face, snapping his head back. The man groaned and lay still. Quickly Justice bound him with the guard's own belt and bandanna, winging his weapons away, stuffing a filthy handkerchief in his mouth.

There was a fire glowing softly in a cave not fifty feet ahead. Somewhere in the shelter of the rocks, the Thunder Riders were resting, planning their next assault on Fist.

The voice was unexpected, nearly startling—a woman's voice came from the cave, and Justice halted, ducking low.

"Where is the damned army? Do we have to finish this ourselves?" Ada Sinclair whined.

Another, soothing voice answered her. Ruff didn't get the words. It sounded like Jesse Todd, trying to calm his wild-eyed murderess.

Ruff glanced up and thought he briefly saw the hem of a woman's dress—in the darkness it was difficult to be sure. The voices faded away and there was nothing but the faint smear of firelight against the rocks, the constant river.

But there was a way up to the cave. Justice had been searching the bluff with his eyes, and now, by starlight, he could make out a series of naturally stepped rocks leading up to the cave's mouth.

Ruff's vision followed them upward to the ledge before the cave. Nothing to it. Nothing to the climb, but what about afterward? How many people were in that cave?

It damned near made his mouth water, knowing that

Ada Sinclair and her henchman, Jesse Todd, were in the same small alcove not sixty feet from where he now stood in the shadows watching, listening.

A Thunder Rider emerged from the cave and started down the tiered rocks. Ruff let this one pass by unmolested. He pressed himself against the face of the bluff and waited, trigger finger tense on the Winchester's receiver as the man strode past. He turned—thank God—in the opposite direction from the one where Ruff had left two men on the ground, one bound, one dead.

Justice looked across the river toward the opposite bluff where Fist counseled with his men and waited for the white forces to crush his people. Ruff had promised the Cheyenne he would do something. He had given his word.

"Just what in hell are you going to do then, Justice?" Ruff asked himself with silent anger.

The night gave him no answer; the river chuckled past, mocking his question.

And Ada Sinclair emerged from the cave.

Ruff's breath caught. He withdrew farther still into the shadows, looking up and down the beach. There she was, in a tan riding skirt, matching jacket, and white blouse. She stood on the ledge and stretched, her mouth gaping in a silent yawn.

And then she started down the stone steps.

She was armed, A little revolver of some kind gleamed in the holster at her waist. Ruff eased his rifle sling over his shoulder and stared at the ledge overhead, silently coaxing the woman on.

"Just a little nearer. Come here, you green-eyed she-devil." Ruff had his bowie in his hand. He crouched, arms dangling, like some savage night creature awaiting its prey.

"Just a little closer."

She was still alone; still no one had appeared on the ledge above. The woman reached the beach and sauntered toward Ruff, a merry little killer without a worry in the world.

Ruff Justice sprang out of the darkness, his hand going over Ada Sinclair's mouth, and as she reached for her little pistol, the point of his bowie dug a fraction of an inch into the smooth, lovely flesh of her throat.

"Draw it," Ruff whispered savagely, "and you'll die."

She shook her head, trying to twist free, but Ruff would have none of it. She tried to kick at his knees, to slam her fist back into his groin, but Justice, jabbing the point of his knife in a little more, brought all that to a halt.

"Shuck the gun, lady," Justice said, and she did it, very slowly, well aware of the deadly steel at her throat. Force was one thing the lady understood.

She knew who had her now; she just didn't know if he would kill her or not. Justice couldn't have said himself at that point. Maybe so, maybe so.

"Keep your finger away from the trigger," Ruff hissed into her ear. "If that thing goes off, you go off—for good. Understand?"

She understood, all right. The pistol rested in her hand for a moment and then was flung away into the willow brush. His eyes still on the cave, Justice turned and dragged the lady down the beach. At first she went passively, nearly limp in Ruff's arms, but as they got farther from the cave, she began to struggle, to kick and flail.

"Stop it or I'll knock you over the head," Ruff told her. The struggling didn't stop immediately, but she seemed to get the idea now that Justice was serious, and gradually she gave it up.

They had gone half a mile from the caves before Ruff took his hand away from her mouth. There was no guarantee that she wouldn't yell and bring help from somewhere, but she seemed resigned.

"I came out of the cave to use the facilities," Ada

Sinclair complained, "and I still have to use the facilities."

"You talk real dainty now, don't you? What happened to that tough, cussing woman I heard at the tent town?"

"I said I had to use the facilities," Ada said stubbornly.

"All right." Justice halted her by yanking on her belt. "Squat, then."

"With you here?"

"It won't work, Ada. You know I'm not that much of a gentleman. You squat. I'll hold your hand."

"Bastard." She said it softly, but Ruff thought he had never heard such venom in a single word. Ada slipped her riding skirt off, almost violently yanked off her bloomers, and squatted, appearing quite indifferent to Ruff's presence.

Ruff watched the river for a moment. The moon was rising now, and that could be good or bad, depending on whether you were the hunter or the hunted.

"Satisfied," Ada Sinclair asked, rising. She reached for her skirt but Justice halted her.

"Forget that, you won't need it. Shed your jacket too."

She gave him a penetrating look, and a small smile began to lift the corners of her mouth. "Sure, Justice. Want me to take my blouse off too? We did have fun, didn't we? That night in Bismarck."

She moved to him, dressed in boots, bloomers, and blouse. She kissed him suddenly, hungrily, her open mouth damp and heated.

Ruff stepped back and spat. "It's not like that, Ada. We're going for a swim."

"A swim! In that?" She looked at the dark river racing past. "You're crazy. It's freezing cold."

"We'll make it. You'll try or I'll drag you by the hair," he told her.

"Like hell you will," she exploded. "I'm not going and you're not going to take me. Why in hell don't you just leave me alone, Justice? Leave me alone and get out of this country yourself while you're still able. What is it, you think you're going to save the Indians or something by holding me hostage? It'll never work, Todd has his orders; he'll kill them all. It won't matter whether I'm there or not. You can't stop the Thunder Riders," she taunted, "no one can now!"

"Don't bet on that," Justice answered. He had taken off his gun belt and slung it around his neck. The river still raged past, the cold moon streaking its turbulent face. "I think they can be stopped. I know just the people to do it."

"Who? That ragged band of filthy Indians?"

"I was thinking of the U.S. cavalry," Ruff said, and Ada just stared at him, defying him with her eyes, the angles of her body.

"Take me to them," she said with a harsh laugh. "Yes, why don't you just do that, Ruff Justice? Take me to them and I'll tell my father and the colonel all about you. How a renegade white scout raped me and then, because this scout, this Ruff Justice, knew that I wanted to find out the truth about Fist's planned uprising, he had his Cheyenne girlfriend try to murder me. I was lucky; I escaped. Another band of Cheyenne warriors found an unlucky saloon girl, and thinking it was me, they murdered her brutally.

"Ruff Justice," Ada said, walking in a small circle now, carried away with her own story, "made his escape—how did you escape anyway?—made his escape and rejoined his Cheyenne friends and proceeded to lead them to several scattered outposts where he butchered and murdered with the best of the Indians."

"Through?" Ruff asked.

"Do you like it? I'm almost through. A respected Washington lobbyist who also happens to be a good friend of mine, Jesse Todd, and I saw that the army was reluctant to act against the Cheyenne. We took it upon ourselves to organize a civilian militia to combat the rapacious Cheyenne. We finally tracked down Fist himself and we had him pinned down until Justice slipped out of the Indian camp and kidnapped me. He tried to rape me again, then threatened me with death unless I went along with him. 'Here I am Father'—this is where I break down into tears, Justice—'take me home, take this scoundrel and have him hung. Oh, yes, Colonel MacEnroe, my men still have Fist pinned down. If you hurry you can catch the bastard and kill him!' "

She stood there, smug and pleased with herself, hands on her hips. "Take me in, Justice. I'll tell my story and you can tell yours. Take me in and we'll see who they'll believe, a woman-killing white renegade scout or a dainty little lady from the East, the daughter of a United States senator."

"You're really twisted, aren't you? I know your mother was killed by Indians, but people get over those things. Some people. I guess you were born mad, Ada. Because you know you're mad now, don't you? No one can hate this long, this hard, without being just plain insane." Ruff nodded. "Come on now."

"Where?" Ada asked in astonishment.

"You asked me to take you to MacEnroe and let you tell your story. That's what I'm going to do."

"And commit suicide!"

"We'll just have to see how it works out," Ruff Justice said. "I've got to at least have my try—it's up to them if they believe your story or not. I've run out of other chances. I'll take this one."

"They'll kill you! I'll see to it. If they don't, I'll do it myself!"

She fought and screamed with Justice all the way to the river's edge. It didn't do her any good. Ruff went in and yanked the woman after him into the cold, dark current, which swept them away.

17

If the river was cold, it was nothing compared to the wind as they emerged on a sandy spit, soaking wet and bone-weary. Ruff sat with his legs drawn up, arms around his knees, breathing in deeply. That damned wound just wouldn't stop throbbing, but then it hadn't been given much of a chance to heal.

Ada Sinclair lay on her back, holding her abdomen and shivering violently. Ruff watched her for a moment, then searched the darkness around them. It wasn't a real good place to be with the moon beaming down. There were Thunder Riders around and probably soldiers as well. A few Cheyenne, perhaps, ready by now to kill anyone with a white face. It didn't give a man a real sense of security.

"You're trying to kill me," Ada moaned. "Why don't you just do it? I'm freezing!"

"Tough." At least she was alive, not lying in her grave or left for the coyotes.

"You called me mad, Justice," she said, rolling over. "Do you know who's mad? It's you. You're trying to stop something that can't be stopped. One day there won't be a single Indian left on these plains, no matter what you do. All you're going to do now is throw your own life away. For nothing!"

Ruff didn't answer. Deep inside he had the feeling that

Ada Sinclair was right, and it was a saddening thought. As enemies or friends, the Indians belonged here, like the wild things, and if the day came when they were all gone, the prairie would seem empty and haunted.

"Come on," Ruff growled. He rose to stand, shaking in his water-logged buckskins.

"You're not going to give up this madness?"

"No. Can't. Besides, I think there's someone out there," Justice answered.

"Someone . . . Who?"

"Could be most anybody right now. Let's not wait around and find out."

"It's my men," she said, rising hopefully to her feet. "It's Hawkins or Deke Connely, or Todd. You're scared! They'll catch you and kill you."

"Maybe. Or maybe it's Cheyenne. If they got their hands on you, they'd make Tate Hawkins' work look like child's play. And I'm not sure now if I could stop them—I'm not even sure I would try. Let's move now. Into the trees."

She still hesitated, and Ruff grabbed her hand, towing her after him into the dark pines, which glowed faintly at their tips with moonlight.

It was a tough climb in soaking-wet clothes. Jutting rocks appeared in their path and they had to clamber up and over them, skinning knees and elbows. The moon was high and hard now, white against a starry sky. Ada dragged behind and Ruff yanked her forward, keeping a viselike grip on her hand, pulling her as she stumbled, faltered, and half-fell.

"Why are we hurrying? Why do we have to go so fast?"

"Lady, if we slow down, people are going to die. When the moon drops behind that ridge, it'll be getting too close to sunrise, and I figure that's when the Thunder Riders are going to try to take the Cheyenne in those caves, or am I wrong?"

She wouldn't answer that.

Ruff simply plodded on, cresting the pine-thick ridge at last.

He stopped abruptly, still holding Ada's hand. There was something on the air, distant and faint. Ruff smiled in the darkness. Coffee. Coffee and the remnants of a dead cookfire. A horse whickered below and was answered by another.

"What is it?" Ada Sinclair asked.

"The army," Ruff said. "Come on."

He had started on when he felt the jerk at his holster and Ada Sinclair stepped back to try to blast his belly out for him. Ruff slammed his fist into her face—her too-lovely face—before she could do it.

Ada dropped the gun and sagged to the pine-needle-littered earth, out cold. Ruff picked up his pistol and holstered it. He shouldered Ada Sinclair and started down the slope, toward the horses and the dead fires.

He reached the flats and walked across the narrow stream. Ada Sinclair was still out cold. The smoke, which he had thought was coming from campfires, had another source. Ahead and to the west was Fist's village. The place had been torched. Ruff walked on grimly, shifting his load.

"Hold it right there or you're dead," a voice said from the darkness.

"Take it easy, Buzz," Justice answered calmly.

The voice was easy to identify. Private First Class Busby Hill had been wounded in the throat, his voice was raspy, breathy.

The soldier stepped out from behind the tree and was joined by two other men, their Springfield rifles raised.

"Mister Justice!"

"It's me, Buzz," Ruff admitted.

"God damn me. I don't believe it!"

The soldier came nearer, eyeing Ruff. He took Ruff's

weapons after Justice nodded approval and then stood, hat tilted back, staring at the half-naked woman on Ruff's shoulder.

"What in blazes are you doing here, Mister Justice?"

"I suppose, Buzz," Ruff said, shifting his load again, "that I'd better see the colonel."

"Yes, sir. I suppose so. We'll kind of escort you along if you don't mind."

Ruff grinned. "I expected you would, Buzz. Is Senator Sinclair along?"

"Yes, sir, he is."

"Good. Might as well get all the fireworks over at once. Did Ray Hardistein get in?"

"Ray? No, sir. I understood he was looking for you up north," the soldier replied as they walked through the burned-out village toward the army camp beyond.

"He was. He found me."

The soldier stopped in his tracks. "He found you—and then let you go? Ray Hardistein?"

"It's a long story, Buzz. We'll talk about it over coffee sometime."

"Yeah," Buzz answered. He sounded as if he didn't think Ruff Justice would be spending much future time sitting around a campfire telling tales. Maybe he was right.

The colonel's tent was on a low knoll by itself. A sentry stood before it. The tent was dark and silent as Justice walked toward it with his escort, feeling Ada Sinclair start to struggle now. He slapped her butt hard and walked on, Buzz Hill still staring at him incredulously.

"It's all right," Ruff said, "the senator's daughter and I have gotten to be friends."

"Yes, sir," Buzz muttered.

The sentry lowered his rifle to a ready position and peered at the new arrivals. "Buzz? What's up?"

"Mister Justice to see the colonel," Buzz answered.

"Justice . . . ?" The sentry looked stunned. "All right. I'll wake him up. For this. Maybe he'll let me stay and listen."

The soldier rapped on the tent's wooden frame and went in. Justice could hear MacEnroe growl something, then a sharp exclamation of surprise. Ada Sinclair wriggled again and Justice slapped her bottom hard again.

The sentry appeared from within as a lantern was lit in the colonel's tent. "Take him in," he told Busby Hill. Then the sentry lit out at a trot.

"Where are you going?" Buzz called after him.

"To get the senator."

Buzz looked at Justice again, then dubiously back at the tent. "Well"—he shrugged—"come on, Mister Justice."

Buzz led the way. Ducking to clear the lintel, Ruff followed him in, two soldiers behind him. The colonel had a cot, a folding chair, and a desk inside—he hadn't been planning on a short campaign, obviously.

He was just hitching up his suspenders, his gray eyes red and dark-ringed, his silver hair rumpled, when Justice entered. The colonel just stared at the scout, shook his head, and reached for his tunic.

"Thank you, Private Busby. Wait outside, please."

"Yes, sir."

"What's that you have there, Justice?" the colonel wanted to know. He was fastening the buttons on his tunic.

"Seems to be the senator's daughter, sir."

"That's what I thought. Put her down, will you?"

Ada's feet touched the floor and she regained her full form instantly. "I demand that you arrest this man, hang him. I demand—"

"Let's wait for your father, shall we, Miss Sinclair?" the colonel interrupted. Under his breath he said, "Quite a lot of demanding from a supposedly dead person."

Confident now of victory, Ada Sinclair went to the

colonel's chair and plopped herself in it. The colonel's eyes narrowed with irritation.

"Here." MacEnroe handed her a blanket to cover herself. "Justice, you look like hell," he said.

"Yes, sir, I guess I do." Ruff looked down at his sleeveless buckskin shirt, his bandaged arm, and well-skinned hands.

"Sit down. I don't want you to drop."

Ruff had barely planted himself on another canvas chair before Senator Cotton Sinclair burst into the room in a blue bathrobe. His face was crimson, his eyes were afire as he glanced at Ruff Justice.

Ada rose and threw herself into his arms, sobbing hysterically. "Oh, Father. He's done terrible things to me. He's a madman. If those soldiers hadn't rescued me, I don't know what would have happened!"

She turned tear-filled, ugly eyes on Ruff Justice, who yawned.

"You snake," the senator exploded, "you low-life bastard!" He approached Justice, fist upraised.

"Remember what I told you last time, Senator," Ruff cautioned him. "Hit me and I'll damn sure hit you back."

The fist still hovered over the senator's head. "You . . ." he began, but he couldn't think of anything despicable enough to call Ruff and he went back to comforting his daughter.

"I want him to hang," Ada Sinclair whimpered. "He deserves it."

"He will hang, damn the man," Senator Sinclair said across his daughter's pathetically heaving shoulder to Colonel MacEnroe, expecting instant agreement.

MacEnroe surprised them. "For what?" the officer asked.

"For what?" The senator was nearly out of control. "Damm it all, you know what this man's done!"

"Yes," Colonel MacEnroe said quietly, letting a bit of

steel enter his voice as he looked at Ada Sinclair. "If I recall, Senator Sinclair, the charge is murdering your daughter."

"Yes, but . . ." the senator blustered a little without any coherent words coming out of his mouth. He looked at his daughter with new curiosity. "Where have you been, Ada? What are you doing with Justice? Dressed like that?"

"How should I be dressed after he ripped my clothes off?" Ada began, moving into her speech. Her eyes were smug and confident as she stared at Justice, walked back to the folding chair, and sat down.

"He's a renegade. He fights with Fist against the whites," Ada said. Colonel MacEnroe stood, expressionless, in the middle of the room. The senator was seething. His daughter had been abused.

"Justice," Ada Sinclair went on, "knew that we were here to find out the truth about the Indian situation. He was afraid that we would discover his role in Fist's plan to massacre every white on the plains . . ."

"That's what we intended to do," Ruff Justice said, and the three people facing him fell silent. Ada's mouth gaped open. "Kill all of the settlers. This land is Fist's. He paid me well." The senator edged toward him, fury and astonishment on his face. Ruff continued, "This is our land. I am an adopted Indian, you know. A Crow. My fight is the same as Fist's. To kill all the whites. To take their women and kill them, to burn their houses, to hack their women into small pieces as the children watch, as—"

"No!" Ada Sinclair leapt from her chair and tried to get her hands on Ruff's neck. The senator held her back. "Killing murdering redskinned bastards! Scum! To kill . . . to kill . . ." Her eyes had glazed over. A bit of spittle had appeared at the corner of her mouth to drool down her chin. "We will kill *them!* We will kill them all. That's why

I organized the Thunder Riders, that's why I wanted the army to . . ."

She had gone a little too far. She halted in midsentence and turned to her father, looking lost and confused.

"Wanted the army to do what, Miss Sinclair?" MacEnroe asked.

"To kill them. To kill every last one." Her voice had become singsong, nearly childish. "You know what they did, Daddy. They took Momma and cut her with their knives. Then they did other things"—she frowned, her forehead furrowing—"nasty things I shan't even say." The fury returned. She beat at her father's chest. "We have to kill them! A race of savages. We have to kill them. We have to kill Ruff Justice. We have to kill . . ."

Her words went on for a while, but no one was listening. The senator held his daughter and looked at Colonel MacEnroe, who waited, stiff and erect, watching.

"I'm sorry, sir," Cotton Sinclair said. He turned toward Justice but was unable to get out an apology. Then with his arm around his daughter, he turned and led the madwoman out into the cold Dakota night.

When they had gone, Mac Enroe asked, "Want to tell me about it now, Ruff?"

"I'd be happy to. If you'll listen."

"I think I'm ready to . . ." The sentry had appeared in the doorway.

"Beg pardon, sir. Patrol coming in."

"Patrol?" The colonel frowned.

"Sergeant Ray Hardistein, sir. And ten men, two wounded."

The colonel looked at Ruff again and Justice said, "Let's allow Ray to make his report first, sir."

"It's tied up with this Sinclair business?" the colonel asked.

"Everything is, sir. It's all tied up with this Sinclair business."

"I see." MacEnroe asked no more questions then. Instead, he walked to his trunk, lifted a bottle of bourbon from among his blankets, and poured a splash of whiskey into his tin cup. Before he had lowered the cup, Ray Hardistein could be heard outside.

"I've got to see the old man now," Ray said excitedly. Then Ray, in a torn and bloodied uniform came inside. He saw Justice and said, "Jesus, Ruff, are you everywhere?" Remembering himself, he saluted, removed his hat, and reported.

When he was through, MacEnroe had a pretty good picture of what was happening on the plains. Justice filled him in a little more and brought things up to the present.

"Fist's holed up in the caves. The Thunder Riders have him pinned down. They're probably hoping the army is going to show up soon and legitimize the slaughter they've got in mind."

"And if the army doesn't arrive?"

"They'll do it anyway, sir, and take their chances."

"Private!" MacEnroe bellowed, and the sentry, who had obviously been listening, poked his head in.

"Yes, sir?"

"How long until sunrise?"

"It's gettin' gray already, sir. Less than an hour."

"Have the bugler sound boots and saddles. Justice! Can we reach the caves in an hour?"

"I think so. We can damn sure try. Don't tell me, sir," Justice said with a grin, "that you're doing this on my say-so, that you're starting to believe me."

"Think I let you down back at Fort Lincoln, Ruffin?" the colonel asked as he reached for his saber and pistol.

"I didn't have the feeling I was getting a lot of support against the senator's charges."

"I don't speak up against a senator—or a general officer—or the President, understand me, Ruffin."

"Yes, sir. You're *army*."

"I'm army." MacEnroe put his hat on and strode toward the door as the bugle outside awakened his soldiers. He paused just a moment before he went outside. Without looking back at Justice, he said, "By the way, if you still have that key to the cell in the stockade, I'd appreciate it if you'd return it. Mine is the only one there is outside of Sergeant Albertson's."

Then the colonel was gone. Ruff stood there a minute, grinning, before he snatched up a spare rifle and followed the officer into the gray morning.

18

The sun was a faint silver presence on the eastern horizon when the army moved out toward the caves along the river bluffs. The colonel was erect and grim, his gray horse stepping out nimbly.

Ruff Justice was back a way, riding beside Ray Hardistein, who, despite the long ride he had just completed, wanted to be in on this. It had gotten personal.

"Thunder Riders jumped us and chased us almost ten miles. We holed up in a buffalo wallow and managed to hold them off until they got tired of it and pulled out. They hit McConnell in the hip. Champ Carlton took one in the belly. It looks bad for Champ, according to the surgeon." Ray paused and looked away, toward the rising sun. "Ruff, sorry it took me so long to believe what you were telling me."

Justice glanced at Colonel MacEnroe, now riding at the head of his men. "Can't be helped, Ray. You're a soldier."

Another thought entered Ray's mind. "The girl, Ada Sinclair, what will they do with her, Ruff? Don't dare hang her, do they? Daughter of a senator like that."

"She won't get hung," Ruff answered. "From what I've seen she'll just be locked up in her own house for the rest of her natural life, locked up in some room snapping at herself like a rabid she-wolf."

The column was closing up, halting in the trees above the bluff. Colonel MacEnroe lifted a gloved hand and waved Ruff to come to him. Justice rode quickly forward.

"This it?" the colonel asked.

"That cluster of caves there, sir. Maybe others. The leaders were in the largest one on your left."

"Hell of an objective for cavalry. Maybe we should have come up the river."

"Not possible on horseback, sir. But," Ruff Justice said, "you've got what you need to do the job."

"Yes." The colonel knew what Ruff meant. He turned in his saddle and said to Lieutenant Hart at his side, "Bring the field pieces up, Hart. Caissons at the ready." MacEnroe squinted into the canyon depths. "Line the cannon at intervals of a hundred feet."

"Yes, sir." Hart saluted and called out, "Artillery officer forward!"

"It's pure murder," MacEnroe said thoughtfully but without much compassion. The Thunder Riders didn't deserve much. "Give them the chance to surrender, Justice?"

"That's more or less your decision, isn't it, sir?"

"What would you do, Justice?"

"Blow them to a waiting hell," Ruff said, unable to keep the emotion out of his voice.

"Yes." The colonel nibbled at the tip of his silver mustache. "Being a civilized man, I'll give them a chance, though. Hate to send a messenger."

"Sir," Ruff said, "what about the Cheyenne?"

"What do you mean? They're safe enough."

"They're safe enough, but they don't know that yet. For all they know you've come after them. Also they have a fear of being punished for killing some of the white Thunder Riders."

"Do you want to talk to them?" MacEnroe asked.

"Not much, but I guess I will."

MacEnroe looked at his scout and turned his head away. The cannon were hastily being set into place, the artillery master gauging his range with a practiced eye.

"Do it quickly, then, Justice. And, Justice, the Cheyenne have no weapons."

"Sir?" Ruff didn't get that one.

"I said these Cheyenne are unarmed. Any Thunder Rider who may be killed today was killed by the U.S. army trying to wipe out a nest of outlaws."

Ruff grinned. "I'll tell Fist, sir."

"Do that. You know, Ruff, we've a chance to start something here today, something worthwhile. Maybe out of Ada Sinclair's crazy dream of slaughter we can begin to build a peace, to see if Fist's dream of peace can't be forged out of this."

That was a long speech for MacEnroe and he fell suddenly silent. He sat his gray horse erect and ready, looking off across the canyon to his objective as his soldiers swung down and crept to the edge of the bluff, rifles ready.

Ruff decided to make his try before the colonel opened up. Finding a rope, he tied knots in it at six-foot intervals, lashed on to a heavy caison, grinned at Ray Hardistein, and started over the edge.

He was hoping that the Thunder Riders wouldn't be looking for someone to come down to the caves from above; and Ruff was expecting MacEnroe to give him all kinds of cover if someone did start sniping.

The wind was fresh, carrying the river's scent as Justice went over the edge of the bluff and started making his way down toward the trail below.

It was an easier descent than that of the night before. Shorter, for one thing, and Ruff could see what he was doing. He was on the trail in two minutes, still having drawn no fire. He glanced up but could see nothing of the soldiers.

He was slightly below the cave where Fist was hidden,

waiting for anything, and Ruff started that way. At first he saw nothing inside the cave, no one, but then he made out the eyes, the eyes and painted faces, the coolly glinting rifle barrels.

"It's me," Ruff Justice said. Rifle muzzles lowered and switched toward Justice. "Get Fist," he said, but no one said a word. They had their warpaint on and they had prepared themselves to die, to make desperate war against the whites. Justice had been a guest; now he was the enemy.

"Dammit all," Ruff said, and he marched right into the cave. Someone grabbed him and hurled him across the cavern. A foot tripped him and he fell to the floor of the cave to sit looking up into the warlike faces of the Cheyenne.

Then Fist was there, his paint making him seem even more powerful, more hostile.

"I told you to run away," Fist said.

Ruff rose, dusting himself off. His eyes were fixed on Fist. From the corner of his eye he noticed Spring Walker. She was holding a rifle, staring at him as if he had returned from the land of the dead.

"Go, now," Fist said, and he turned his back.

Justice said, "I can't. There are soldiers all along the bluff above us, Fist. They've got four cannons with them."

Fist spun angrily toward Justice. "You have brought them to us!"

"Just think of what I said, dammit, Fist! I said they're above us. You know they can't attack you here from there. They don't mean to. They want the Thunder Riders. In a few minutes it's going to begin."

"You lie!"

"Me? No," Ruff said, "I don't lie. You know that, or it wouldn't have been me you sent for once. I've talked to Colonel MacEnroe, the white war leader. This time, he says, you're on the same side, fighting for peace, against the Thunder Riders . . ."

Fist couldn't accept those words, and he simply stared at Justice. From above them a rifle was fired and then another. Fist's eyes flashed to the cave mouth. His warriors started in that direction, cocking their weapons.

"Wait!" Ruff called out. He touched Fist's arm. "Wait just one minute.

"We will kill them all."

"The Thunder Riders, yes. MacEnroe said to tell you this: the Cheyenne have no guns today. If any white is killed, the soldiers have done it. Do you understand me, Fist?"

"No, I do not understand." Another volley was fired from above. Fist walked to the mouth of the cave, grim and resolute. Ruff went with him. Someone was yelling from above them, and now, reaching the mouth of the cave, they could hear MacEnroe himself calling into the canyon.

"You in the caves! This is Colonel MacEnroe, U.S. army. Throw down your weapons and come out of there. Come out now or pay the consequences."

No one emerged from the opposite caves. Jesse Todd and Hawkins knew they couldn't come out, couldn't give it up. There was a hanging rope waiting for each man. Maybe if they had known about the cannon, they might have come out, but they didn't know and they decided to take on the army.

A shot and then another were touched off from across the way, bullets flying toward the top of the bluff. MacEnroe could be heard shouting an indistinct order and then all of the smaller sounds were overwhelmed by the bellowing of cannon. The first ball was low, the second high, sending clouds of red dust into the air. The third was a direct hit on one of the caves and the Cheyenne cheered.

Fist looked at Justice as if the scout had played a dirty trick on him by telling the truth. Then, rapidly, he ordered his warriors to begin firing.

The cave was filled with the deafening sound of the repeating rifles sending their bullets toward the caves opposite. Powder smoke settled heavily in the cave as brass cartridges ejected by the repeaters littered the floor.

From above the army rifles opened up, sharp, methodical, punctuated at intervals by the heavy boom of a cannon and the soft hum of a ball passing over, striking stone and bringing death across the river.

The Thunder Riders had no choice and soon they made their break for it. The Cheyenne riflemen cut them down, sent them tumbling down the bluffs or into the river to bob away in the current.

Ruff saw one man make it to his horse, which was held in a small feeder canyon, and ride hell for it up the brushy ravine. Searching rifle fire failed to stop him and he was up and out of the gorge, safe for the time being.

The rifle fire was as loud as the thunder of hell, continuous. Still a few of the Thunder Riders, not bothering to fire back, managed to reach their horses. One of them was dropped from his mount's back by a sharpshooter—Cheyenne or army—but two others managed to make their way out of the canyon.

Ruff watched them through the powder smoke. There didn't seem to be anything anyone could do to stop this handful of men. They had been fortunate enough to have been in the right cave, near the horses, fortunate enough to have made their way through the hellfire of the guns.

Then Justice saw them. At first he didn't recognize Hawkins, not at that distance, but at any distance it was difficult to miss the bearlike proportions of Deke Connely. There was another man with them—Jesse Todd?

Ruff took a step forward, watching intently. They dipped into the willow brush and worked their way at a run toward the ravine where the horses were.

"They're going to make it," Justice said aloud. "Going to get clear."

The hell they were.

Ruff Justice touched Fist's arm. "I'm going out. Give me a second to get past your guns."

The boom of a cannon drowned out a part of his words. Fist shook his head, sighting down his rifle barrel. Ruff grabbed the Cheyenne war leader's arm.

"I said I'm going out! Their leaders are getting away."

Fist saw Ruff's hand on his arm and his anger flared up briefly. But then he nodded, shouting to his men to hold their fire. Justice ducked out of the cave and started down the trail at a run. Someone saw him—a single bullet flew past, impacting against the bluff face—but the men across the way had other things to worry about. With the continuous fire keeping their heads down. Justice drew no more fire.

The foot of the trail was just too far down. Ruff paused, looked below, and leapt feet first toward the river. He knifed through the icy, fast-moving water and touched bottom. Coming up again, he began stroking, swimming toward the opposite bank, turning his head from side to side. Above him the war went on.

Ruff dragged himself up and out of the water. Sopping wet, he ran through the willows toward the ravine mouth above him. A poorly aimed cannon round struck stone not fifty feet above Justice, and the impact knocked him to the ground, showering him with dust.

Justice covered up reflexively, arms over his head. No second ball struck near and so he scrambled to his feet and ran on.

Bill Whitney suddenly appeared before him. In the confusion of the day Whitney took a moment to remember whether Ruff was a friend or an enemy.

He took just a little too long. Ruff leapt at the outlaw, driving his knife into the man's gut. Whitney flopped back, quivering, his single eye glaring at the empty sky.

Ruff winged his own pistol away. Maybe the swim

hadn't ruined it, but Whitney's was certainly dry and loaded. He ripped the Winchester from Whitney's dead fingers and ran on, his breath coming harshly, up the slope and toward the outlaw horses, which were milling and rearing in panic.

Ruff found a good one—a long-legged, deep-chested bay—and swung aboard. His bowie slashed at the long rope the other animals were tethered to, and he hied them up and out of the ravine. Justice rode on, flagging the bay with his rifle, urging it on to full speed up a rocky, nopal-cactus-cluttered slope.

Then Justice was out of the canyon, riding free across a barren bluff rim.

And ahead of him three men rode desperately southward, their little kingdom of murder falling apart behind them.

Justice took the reins in his left hand, shouldered Whitney's rifle, and fired four times. One bullet tagged home. Tate Hawkins bounced from his horse's back and landed on his neck.

Todd and Deke Connely turned their heads toward him, Connely opening up with a handgun as his horse dipped into a wash and scrambled up the far side.

Justice heeled his horse on, flapping the stirrups against its flanks. He reached the wash half a minute behind Deke Connely and drew up sharply as he did so, realizing that Todd hadn't emerged from the wash at all.

Ruff looked right, but the bullet came from his left, and the bay went down, throwing Justice free. The rifle flew into the tangled brush, and Justice, kicking free of the stirrups, leapt after it, another bullet singing past him and clipping brush.

The day went still. The gunfire behind them was only a distant murmur. The humming of the insects in the brush was nearly as loud. Cicadas buzzed in a raucous primitive chorus. And then fell silent.

But someone was disturbing them, moving forward through the deep manzanita and sumac, toward Justice, who lay, breathing hard, dust in his nostrils, Colt .44 revolver in his hand. Holding one hand over the hammer to muffle the sound, he heeled the hammer back and waited, eyes shifting from point to point, trying to penetrate the mesh of the brush.

He came from behind Ruff Justice. Jesse Todd reared up triumphantly and lifted his rifle to his shoulder. Justice rolled onto his back and fired.

The two weapons went off simultaneously, Todd's bullet striking the earth beside Justice's head, stinging him with the gravel it kicked up.

Justice's bullet struck flesh. Jesse Todd was spun around, a womanly scream rising from his throat as he grabbed at his shoulder, his rifle flying free.

Ruff got unsteadily to his feet. He walked to where Todd lay writhing in pain. The look on his face was tortured and astonished.

This couldn't be happening to him—not Jesse Todd. Ruff stood over the outlaw for a long while before he realized he was enjoying it. Shaking away that mood, he crouched to see how bad it was.

And the bear burst from the brush behind him, the great bearded bear who growled as he hurled himself at Ruff, slamming him to the earth. Both men rolled across Jesse Todd and into a sandy clearing. Ruff came up first, reaching for his sidearm, but it was gone.

Deke Connely stood before him, massive chest rising and falling in primitive exultation. He had his man now, had him, and he was going to finish what he had started. He was going to rip Justice limb from limb, tear his head off and stomp on it.

He was grinning as he came in, grinning with the glee of a blood-crazed predator.

The arrow from the brush took Deke Connely in the

back and he slapped at it. His eyes glazed over and he fell forward, like a giant redwood falling to the earth.

Spring Walker came forward, bow in hand. "This one again. Why did you not kill him, Ruff Justice?"

"I don't know . . . some kind of mental block," Justice said. He was crouched over Deke Connely. "We won't have to worry about it anymore. He's dead now. Good and dead."

"The other one?" Spring Walker asked, and they walked to Jesse Todd, who was rolling around the ground, cursing and sobbing.

"He'll make it to the scaffold. Is it over back there, Spring Walker?" Ruff asked.

"All over. What will happen now, I do not know, but that is over. This one," she asked, casting a contemptuous glance at Jesse Todd, "what shall we do with him?"

"Tie up his wounds, I guess. Bind him and take him to the army."

"And then?" Spring Walker asked, her dark eyes growing softer as she stepped closer to Ruff Justice. "And then what will we do, man of legend?"

Ruff Justice laughed out loud and drew the Indian girl to him, holding her for a long while before they turned their attention to the small defeated man on the ground.

WESTWARD HO!

The following is the opening section from the next novel in the gun-blazing, action-packed new Ruff Justice series from Signet:

RUFF JUSTICE #28: THE LADY WAS AN OUTLAW

1

It wasn't so hard for the messenger to find Ruff Justice. What was difficult was prying him away from the Cheyenne girl he was staying with up along the Arrowhead in that grassy valley where the lone tepee stood.

The corporal was new to Fort Lincoln and he hadn't heard much about its civilian scout, a long, lean man with dark, shoulder-length hair and a drooping mustache, with cold blue eyes and a deadly reputation.

The corporal's name was Doakes and he had been sent by his commanding officer to bring the scout back to Fort Lincoln for duty. To Doakes, a man with six years of faithful service, that meant you brought the man back.

He hadn't encountered anyone like this Justice.

Doakes swung down in the meadow, stretched his back a little, and walked to the tepee. He lifted the tent flap and ducked his head inside, and a voice barked, "Knock, damn you!"

Excerpt from THE LADY WAS AN OUTLAW

Doakes backed out automatically and stood looking at the tepee, trying to figure out where you knocked on the damn things. From inside he thought he heard a woman giggle.

He knocked finally on a tent pole, bringing forth only a muffled sound. Then he ducked his head and started to enter once more.

"No one said 'come in.' Get back out of here." The voice snapped from the darkness and Doakes backed out again hastily. Again a woman giggled and Doakes felt the tips of his ears begin to burn.

Dammit all, he had been sent here to do a job. No one was going to push him around. Tugging down his cap purposefully, the angular, freckled corporal started forward once more.

"Hey, I'm looking for Ruff Justice," the corporal shouted.

That brought no answer at all except for that infernal giggling. Doakes was getting angry, and he was humiliated despite himself by his attempts to get the scout to report to the colonel.

"Come out now, or I'll have to come in and get you," Doakes called in.

"Anyone with you?" a man's voice answered.

Doakes looked around as if he couldn't remember. "No," he answered. He had gone so far as to unbutton the flap on the service holster he was wearing.

"Then you'd better wait for me to come out, son. You don't want to try coming in to get me."

Doakes hadn't been called son by anyone for five years, and he didn't like it. But this time something told him he'd better let it slide by. Maybe he had better just wait.

He waited and he waited some more. The sun was warm, the scent rising from the green grass rich and clean. Inside the tepee a woman giggled and then made a softer, more contented sound. Doakes frowned and looked toward the far hills.

It was half an hour before his quarry emerged. The scout, clad in buckskins, was much taller than Doakes had thought. He had his long dark hair brushed back across his shoulders; he wore a white hat with two hawk feathers in it. At his hip was a Colt .44 revolver with staghorn grips. In his right hand was a .56-caliber Spencer repeater in a beaded buckskin sheath.

He didn't look like a man to fool with, but he grinned when he saw Doakes, and Doakes smiled back automatically.

"Haven't been out here long, have you?" Ruff Justice asked.

"Long enough," the corporal answered in a confident voice that betrayed him by squeaking at the end of his brief statement.

From the tepee a woman emerged, a young Cheyenne girl with hair to her waist. She had a blanket wrapped around her, and unless Doakes was wrong, that was all she was wearing. She glanced at the corporal without interest, then went to Justice and kissed him. Doakes turned his head away.

His head was still turned when a hand fell on his shoulder, a strong tanned hand belonging to the scout.

"Ready now?" Justice asked, and Doakes said that he figured he was. "What's happening?" the scout wanted to know.

Doakes, who had no idea, said confidentially, "I'll leave it to the colonel to tell you, sir."

Ruff started toward his horse, a big buckskin with a dark splotch on its right flank. Then he stopped in his tracks and went back to the Indian girl. He swept her to him with one arm and kissed her again.

The girl beamed with pleasure. "Good-bye, man of legend," Doakes heard her say, and then Justice went to his saddled horse, swinging easily aboard. He nodded to the corporal.

"Let's see what MacEnroe wants," Justice said.

Mounting his army bay, the corporal caught up with Justice and rode with him toward the head of the valley. Behind, the blanket-clad Cheyenne girl watched silently, her hair blowing in the breeze.

Doakes watched her for a minute, then, feeling the scout's eyes on him, he blushed. It was ridiculous, but he blushed. He had endured a great deal of embarrassment while doing a simple task, and it rankled Doakes. By the time they had reached Fort Abraham Lincoln on the Missouri River, however, Doakes' resentment had drifted away. Justice had told him a tale or two, once sang a song, and all in all treated Doakes as if he were his oldest friend in the world.

It wasn't until they had entered Fort Lincoln and Justice had swung down in front of the orderly room that Doakes had time to wonder about the man he had brought in. Hell, Ruff Justice was a fine fellow, he decided in the end.

But in the back of his mind, Doakes also knew he wouldn't ever want to be the scout's enemy.

Ruff Justice gave no further thought to Corporal Doakes as he tramped up the plank steps to the orderly room, swung the heavy door open, and walked in to find Sergeant Mack Pierce pinning up a duty roster on the bulletin board. A duty corporal lifted one sleepy eye and went back to his dreams. Pierce turned his three hundred pounds of flesh slowly toward Justice.

Excerpt from THE LADY WAS AN OUTLAW

"Ruffin," the NCO said familiarly, "how's everything?"

"Could be better. I wasn't quite ready to come back to duty," Justice said.

"I'll bet not." Pierce winked.

"What's up? Not Stone Eyes, I hope."

"No, that bastard has lit out for Canada—for good, I hope." Pierce shook his head. The renegade Indian had given them more trouble in the past year than any six Sioux bands.

Ruff was going to ask another question, but the door to the inner office opened and the tall, silver-haired, mustached man with the eagles on his uniform appeared in the doorway.

Colonel MacEnroe looked stiff and unhappy; Justice grinned. The commanding officer of Fort Lincoln, Dakota Territory, was in a good mood. He wasn't breathing fire and his face wasn't set into a stony disapproving mask; his color was less than crimson.

MacEnroe inclined his head and disappeared into his office. Ruff followed, closing the door behind him.

The colonel stood behind his desk, erect and military. The bottle at his right hand wasn't exactly military, but then even MacEnroe had some human elements. He poured a short drink as Ruff watched.

"How're negotiations with Fist going, sir?" Ruff asked. Fist was a Cheyenne warlord who had come looking for peace and found war. Eventually things had gotten straightened out, up to a certain point.

"People from Washington have come in to handle that. They'll screw it up," the colonel said with the judgment of a man who had lived a good part of his life on the plains, fighting and pacifying the Indian. "That's not what I called you in for, Ruffin."

Excerpt from THE LADY WAS AN OUTLAW

The colonel finished his drink, looked at the empty glass, and tucked it away. He leaned forward, clasping his hands together on his desk.

"What, then, sir?" Ruff asked.

"Cattle."

Justice half-turned in his wooden chair as if the colonel were talking to someone else and Justice was looking for him.

"Maybe we don't understand each other, sir," Ruff said finally.

"A cattle drive. I need someone to guide one in. You're the man, Justice."

"I'm not a cowboy," Justice said flatly. "You don't see any rust on my pistol." MacEnroe knew what Ruff meant but ignored it. There were cowhands, and many of them, who wore their sidearms only for show, wore them so long and through so much foul weather that the things couldn't have been fired without blowing the owner's head off. "And I don't own a pair of chaps."

"I'm not asking you to brand them or cut them or even eat them," MacEnroe said, growing just a little testy. Ruff seemed willing to do almost anything to stay with Spring Walker up in that little meadow. The trouble was the army was still paying this man. "I'm asking you to guide a trail herd to Dakota from Colorado."

"Asking?" Ruff asked dryly.

The colonel ignored that too. "You know Colorado, you know this territory—better than any man I know," the colonel said in a rare compliment, "and you know the country in between. We've a need for a man to bring this herd through. Besides," the colonel said, leaning back in his chair, "I happen to know that you have worked cattle—just after the war, in Texas."

Ruff frowned. No one knew that. No one.

Excerpt from THE LADY WAS AN OUTLAW

"And you once brought a Mexican herd up to Fort Sumner down south. That wasn't too long ago. You know enough to do the job, Justice. You're the only man I have who does know enough."

Justice obviously wasn't happy with this one. He asked, "Just what in hell does the army have to do with bringing a herd of cattle north, and where are they being driven?"

MacEnroe told him. "They are army beef, already paid for. A good deal of the meat is going to end up on our tables. Buffalo aren't so plentiful as they once were, and with winter coming the riverboats will soon be frozen out. The army needs beef, but that's not the whole of it, Justice. There's a good chance we're finally going to make our peace with Fist and his Cheyenne band. A part of the deal we're offering him is food for his people. Cattle.

"They'll be held up at Clear Creek Canyon by the contractor until—and if—the treaty can be finalized with Fist. In any event, the army needs a share of that beef—or we will, by the time the herd can reach Dakota. We'll be butt up against winter by then. If the herd has to be delayed until next spring, the army can hold out; there's rations to be had. However, if we don't have beef to offer Fist to hold his band over the winter, I don't think there's a chance he'll sign the peace treaty. He'll drift south, following the buffalo, and we may miss the only opportunity we'll ever have to enter profitable negotiations with a renegade we've been trying long and hard to bring to the peace table."

"I see." Ruff had his hat on his crossed knee. He turned it now, toying with the two orange-and-black hawk feathers in the band. "It's more important than it sounded, I apologize."

"Ruff Justice apologizing to me!" MacEnroe's mock astonishment caused Ruff's mouth to turn down.

Excerpt from THE LADY WAS AN OUTLAW

"I'll do my best, sir," he said rather formally. "Colorado, is it? Denver?"

"That's right. The herd's being held there—assuming it's arrived."

"Arrived from where?" Ruff asked.

"All the way from Texas, Justice. This is one of the longest and most brutal drives the West has seen yet. The owner is a hell of a trail boss, apparently. What makes it more remarkable is that the owner is a woman. You'll meet this Sylvia Clanton in Denver and . . ." The colonel broke off.

Ruff Justice was leaning forward, his eyes narrow, his expression incredulous. "Sylvia Clanton?" he asked slowly.

"Yes." The colonel blinked and half-shrugged. "Don't tell me you know her, Justice."

"Know her," Ruff Justice answered. "Hell, yes, I know her—the lady is an outlaw."

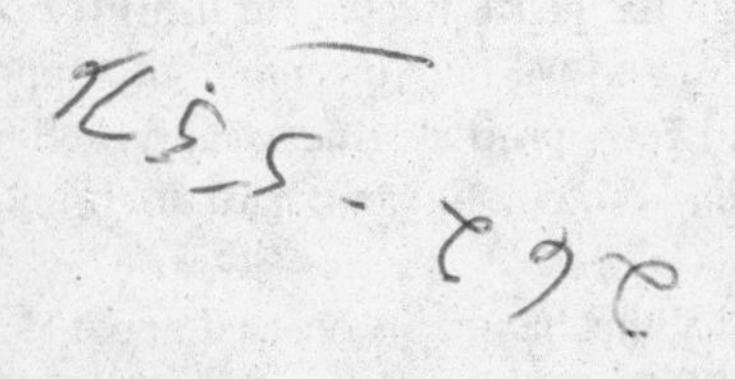